KIDNAPPED BY THE SEAL

HERO FORCE BOOK SEVEN

AMY GAMET

1

Noah Ryker stood on the fourth-floor balcony overlooking the Atlantic, staring into the eerie purple abyss that had taken over the sky. If he had any sense, he'd be anywhere but Hilton Head Beach, South Carolina, dead center in the eye of the storm.

Sense is over-fucking-rated.

He hadn't had any good sense in weeks, might never have it again. Funny how that worked when your world came crashing down around you, bringing you to your knees with a guttural cry. The things that used to mean everything became transparent wisps of nothing, no longer strong enough to tether you down.

Nothing could hold him down anymore.

This moment, this place, this face-off with reality. This was where he needed to be, in his sister's apartment high above the waves, the last place he'd seen her alive just a few months ago. His mother's voice on the phone would haunt him until the end of time.

It's Lizzie.

Oh, Noah...

He closed his eyes, the whipping wind carrying the faint taste of saltwater to his tongue. Those words had sliced his world in half, excising everything that mattered from the flesh and blood left behind.

His baby sister was gone.

In his mind she was eight or nine, clinging to his back as he carried her, lanky colt-like legs wrapped around his hips, barefooted as always, her laughter bubbling over his shoulder like a babbling brook.

He lifted his beer to his lips, taking a long pull deep into his gut. The brew tasted better than any ever had before it, his brain knowing this concoction held the magic that would take him to a place where he could grieve.

Rolling thunder had him opening his eyes, staring into the swirling darkness as if he were staring into the eyes of God himself, and in that moment he hated Him with a fiery passion that was mirrored only in the violence of the storm.

It was a category five named Oscar, about to make landfall right where he was standing, and all Noah could think was, *Bring it on, you fucking bastard.*

He was going to need more beer.

He drained the last of the bottle and walked inside. There were sheets of plywood for covering the glass and bags upon bags of groceries, enough to last him weeks if need be. Even an inflatable boat he'd snagged from HERO Force. As always, he was prepared for any eventuality, figuring the worst that could happen was he'd miss a week or two of work. But after his parting words with Cowboy, that wouldn't be a problem.

I can't even think about that shit right now.

He bent and opened the refrigerator, peering inside, hopeful Lizzie had kept a stash. No beer, damn it. He wasn't much of a drinker and hadn't bought any at the store in

Atlanta, thinking getting drunk was a bad idea. Now he knew better.

Getting drunk was a fantastic idea.

He closed the fridge. There, on a magnet in front of him, was a newspaper clipping.

Joseph Fielding, age 34, died unexpectedly on December 18. A pediatrician, Joe received his M.D. from New York University...

Noah narrowed his eyes. Who was this man to his sister? A lover? A friend? As far as he knew, Lizzie wasn't seeing anyone. He scanned the obituary.

...survived by his wife, Hannah (Grimes) Fielding, and loving son, Brady.

Not a lover, then. At least he sure hoped not. He read the piece more carefully, noting Dr. Fielding previously worked at the same hospital his sister did.

Mystery solved. A coworker, then.

He wondered briefly if Dr. Fielding's family was dealing any better with his death than Noah was with his sister's. Probably not.

He grabbed his wallet and keys. He'd passed a little bodega a few miles up the road on his way in that still had its lights on. He hoped it was open. They were bound to be out of bread and milk—hell, probably beer, for that matter —but when a man was dying of thirst, he had to check any riverbed, even if it might be dry.

He turned toward the door and stopped in his tracks. There was a stretch of hardwood in the living room where carpeting should have been. He hadn't noticed it on his way in, his arms laden with supplies. But now all he could do was stare at it, the idea of Lizzie lying dead setting his imagi- nation on fire.

He pushed out of the apartment, slamming the door on that picture and the reality he refused to accept.

Definitely need more beer.

He took the stairs two at a time to the parking garage beneath. The elevator was an unnecessary risk, one he hadn't even taken while hauling the plywood. The power was going to go out, it was just a question of when, and he sure as fuck didn't want to be trapped in a little box while all of Hilton Head Island was under a mandatory evacuation.

Not that the authorities had the power to make people leave. It was a free country, and he could wait the storm out here if he wanted to. There just wouldn't be any emergency services available if he needed them. He'd heard on the radio on the way in the hospital was closing soon, police and EMTs having already gone off duty. Fortunately for him, he could take plenty good care of himself.

Even if I couldn't save my sister.

It was raining hard and his wipers worked as quickly as they could to keep the windshield free of water, but it was an impossible task and he squinted at the road beyond. Palm trees bent precariously in the wind, their silhouettes against the stormy sky like harbingers of terrible things to come, but all he could think was it should always look like this, every moment of every day since his sister died, the outer world finally matching the turmoil inside him.

Through the rain he glimpsed a white commercial truck pulled to the side of the road. He slowed to a crawl to see if assistance was needed, belatedly realizing a police car sat in front of the truck with its lights off. Several men were climbing in and out of the truck, and he imagined they were abandoning the vehicle and attempting to get their inventory out of it.

He pulled in behind them and stepped into the rain, his head and body instantly soaked with water. "You guys need a hand?"

One man turned and stared at him just as a flash of lightning illuminated his face. Wide forehead, receding hairline, heavy beard. "No."

Noah turned to see the others facing him in a small line, another flash of lightning like someone turning a light on and off. The men wore uniforms—three matching blue with dark pants and one policeman, but it was their expressions that had the hair on the back of Noah's neck standing up.

They wanted him to go away.

Noah held up his hand in a curt wave and turned back to his car. Maybe the men had stumbled upon the abandoned truck and were looting its contents. Mother Nature's tantrums brought out the best in most people, but the underbelly of society was always on the lookout for a quick buck. Or maybe he had it all wrong—one was a cop, after all.

He pulled back onto the road, continuing toward the lights of the bodega in the distance, but only got halfway there before he saw police lights in his rearview mirror. He sighed heavily and pulled to the side of the road, prepared for the inevitable discussion of the mandatory evacuation orders in place and his own right to stay wherever the hell he wanted to weather the storm.

I just want a goddamn beer.

He put his window down, the monsoon-like rains cold on his already soaked body. "Is there something I can do for you, officer?"

"License and registration."

He took them out of his wallet and handed them to the cop, who turned and walked back to his vehicle. Noah's mind went to the five firearms in his pickup truck. There was one in a holster at his waist, another under the seat, and three rifles in cases in the back. All registered, and of course he was licensed to carry, but a simple traffic stop had the potential to get a hell of a lot more complicated if he needed to disclose they were here.

Sniper problems.

The light returned to his window. "Get out of the car, sir."

"I have a firearm holstered at my waist, officer."

The sound of the cop pulling his weapon and releasing the safety was like a drum roll in Noah's head. A prelude to what, he had no idea.

"Keep your hands where I can see them and get out of the truck."

Noah lifted his hands and got out, the wind catching the truck door and slamming it past its natural open angle.

The cop shined the flashlight in Noah's face. "Hands on the vehicle."

He complied, the officer quickly taking his weapon. "What seems to be the problem, officer?" he repeated calmly.

"You are aware that this area is under mandatory evacuation order from the governor?"

"Yes, sir. I've chosen to stay in my home."

"According to your license, your home is in Atlanta."

"I have a condo here."

"Where, exactly?"

Noah rattled off the address as thunder cracked and rolled. "I thought the precinct closed more than an hour ago."

"How about you tell me why you stopped back there?"

"I thought somebody might be in trouble."

"So you were just being a good Samaritan, is that right?"

"Trying to be, yeah."

"You can turn around now, sir."

"Thanks. I thought maybe that medical supply truck was having mechanical problems or something. With the storm coming, I just figured it was better to stop than keep going."

Thunder rolled and the rain came down harder, the drops now covering his skin constantly like a faucet. He stared at the lights of the bodega. Any second now this douche was going to stop pulling his chain and let him get back in his truck, and Noah could only hope that store would still be open when he did.

"The medical supply truck," said the officer. "Did you get a good look at the guys?"

"Just one, and you."

The officer was quiet a beat too long, one single moment for Noah to realize something was wrong. Lightning flashed, illuminating the sky and the officer's face once more. This time, a chill went through Noah's body. He had seen too much. "Look, I didn't see anything. You've got nothing to worry about from me, okay?"

He pictured the gun beneath the truck's bench seat. If he opened the driver-side door, this guy would have his firearm pointed at Noah's brain before he had one hand under the seat. Right at that moment, lightning struck over the officer's shoulder, catching Noah's attention. With a moment's inspiration, he called, "Look out!"

The officer turned to look behind him and Noah ran behind the truck, opening the passenger-side door and grabbing his weapon from beneath the seat. The pop of the officer's gun had Noah instantly in combat mode, experience and memories of wartime fire focusing his senses on the situation at hand. "What's the matter?" asked Noah. "I wasn't supposed to see that?"

"You should have left when you were told to go."

He clucked his tongue. "I'm well within my rights to stay."

"Then you should have minded your own damn business." He fired again, the tire next to Noah instantly deflating.

Noah considered firing back at the officer, but the implications of such a shot were screaming in his brain. He hesitated. This wasn't a war. It wasn't even a HERO Force assignment. It was plain old real life with real-life implications for attacking someone in law enforcement.

He didn't want to hurt this guy, and he sure as hell didn't want to kill him. The officer was shooting out his tires, making it so he couldn't escape. He hadn't taken a shot directly at Noah.

"Damn shame what happened down in Hilton Head, did you hear?" asked the cop. "Some dumb-ass white tourist pulled a gun on a cop during a routine traffic stop." He laughed and fired again. A burning took over Noah's left thigh. He'd been hit.

His third gunshot wound. One in Iraq, one in Afghanistan, now this. A fucking traffic stop in the middle of Hilton Head Island. He wasn't just trying to keep Noah from escaping.

This cop wanted him dead.

Killing a cop would make him an enemy of the state. One pull of his trigger finger could change his entire life. There'd be no more HERO Force. There would be jail time, or worse. South Carolina had the death penalty and there wasn't a damn thing at this scene to back Noah up if the cop went down.

Do you want to live, or do you want to die?

Another bullet whizzed by his ear. Running would make him an easy target. He needed to act, no matter the consequences. Decision made, he concentrated on aiming his weapon, a careful shot into the other man's shoulder that would be extremely painful but wasn't likely to kill. But the cop moved quickly, coming around the vehicle, firing his weapon, and Noah's focus shifted to a kill shot.

He pulled the trigger.

The cop fell to the ground like he'd tripped over a wire.

Noah's breath was coming hard, the sound mixing with the rain pummeling the asphalt. He stood, moving to the cop and checking his neck for a pulse. Nothing.

His eyes raked over the stormy landscape, nothing in sight but that damn same bodega. He was standing in a torrential downpour in fifty-five-mile-per-hour winds, about to go through a hurricane, and now he was a cop killer.

"Fuck, fuck, fuck!" He went back to his truck and grabbed a flashlight, then unbuckled his belt and pulled his pants down to his knees. A hole in the top of his thigh was bleeding profusely. He reached around back, finding a matching hole four inches below where his thigh met his ass. He'd never be able to stitch it himself.

He grabbed a length of paracord from the glove box, tucked neatly between nineteen other carefully chosen items that could be used in a multitude of situations. He tied it as tightly as he could just above the entry and exit wounds. It would buy him some time, but not much of it. He was losing blood quickly and needed his injuries repaired.

He sat in his truck. His eyes closed a beat too long before he pulled out his cell phone and dialed 911. Surely someone was answering emergency calls, even if they couldn't dispatch someone to his location. He tried not to let himself consider what would happen to him now as he dialed.

CALL FAILED.

He squinted at the bars in the corner of the screen. No

SERVICE. He threw the phone hard against the dash. "Goddamn it!"

He had no transportation and a bullet wound to his leg. His eyes went to the police cruiser. He could take it, but for how long? The next passerby could come at any moment or not for days, but when they did, whoever was driving that cruiser would be public enemy number one.

How far would he have to go to find an open hospital? Maybe a hundred miles. He'd be dead by then.

He turned his head in the opposite direction, the lights of the bodega standing out against the storm like a beacon. Someone was inside. Someone who might be able to help instead of him dying alone in the rain. He considered taking the cruiser to the bodega but dismissed the idea. He didn't want the worker at the bodega to go on high alert.

He moved to the back of the truck and grabbed his go bag, slinging it over his shoulder. Inside were the medical supplies that could fix his injury—if only he could reach it —along with everything he needed to survive virtually any situation, at least initially.

It was important to be prepared, but sometimes life threw you curveballs all the preparation in the world couldn't fix.

He limped off toward the bodega in the rain.

2

D r. Hannah Fielding had just finished up an unprecedented thirty-seven-hour shift at Hilton Head Hospital. Pitching her body forward into the wind, she made her way to her car, her scrubs wet and plastered to her body. The microscope she carried was heavy in her arms. She was bone-tired, a weariness like she'd never before experienced suddenly replacing the adrenaline rush that had kept her going for the last day and a half.

She'd been responsible for the well-being of every patient in that hospital, for getting them transferred somewhere inland capable of weathering the storm that could handle each person's individual problems. She sighed heavily. Director Patel should have taken on more responsibility, but instead he'd placed it all firmly in Hannah's lap. And while she was proud of everything she'd accomplished at work, she was overwhelmed by her own lack of preparedness at home for the storm that had been growing outside the hospital windows.

She had to get to her son, Brady. Guilt clawed at her for

leaving him with her in-laws for so long, but what choice did she have? Her phone was full of messages and voice mails from her mother-in-law, Theresa, not-so-patiently waiting for her to leave work.

The rain pelted her face and body, a moment's weakness making her wish so desperately her life had turned out differently. If she'd known she was going to be a single mother, she never would've gone to medical school. Joe had encouraged her, even after she had the baby, but it wasn't a job that let her be there for her son, and now she was all he had.

The close crack of thunder made her jump. She hated storms and would have liked nothing better than to evacuate during this one. But she was a healer, her occupation requiring she run toward danger instead of away from it.

Just let me get Brady home safely. That's all I ask.

She envisioned empty grocery store shelves and cursed as she climbed into her little car. She was sure she had enough dry and canned goods to get them through, but the window of opportunity to buy bread and milk had long since passed.

The dashboard lit. She had less than a quarter tank of gas.

Great.

Enough to make it to her in-laws' house across the island and back home, but talk about being unprepared for a disaster. She wanted to cry, fatigue bearing down, but didn't have the energy to waste on self-pity.

All she had to do was stand her ground, camp out in the condo she shared with Brady while Oscar passed overhead, and hope for the best. She drove slowly through the empty streets of Hilton Head, the roads littered with branches, until she pulled into the circular drive of her in-laws' house and ran to the door.

Back in the day they had loved her.

Joe's parents had welcomed her into their family with open arms. Theresa in particular had been wonderful, so proud of her new daughter-in-law, the doctor. But their dynamic had become terribly strained after Joe died, with Theresa becoming more and more critical of Hannah and the choices she made raising Brady.

They loved their grandson and took good care of him, and for that Hannah was grateful. And if it meant she was on the receiving end of a lot of flack from her mother-in-law on a regular basis, then she would take Theresa's snide remarks with a smile to keep her son happy.

Theresa pulled the door open as if she'd been standing there, waiting for Hannah to arrive, which she probably had. "I was starting to think we wouldn't have time to evacuate. We almost decided to go and bring Brady with us."

She wouldn't take the bait. "I'm here now."

"The eye wall is only forty miles offshore, Hannah. You could have given us a little more time."

"The patients—"

"Oh, leave her alone, Theresa." She turned to her father-in-law, Tom, his features so much like Joe's she sometimes found it hard to look at him. Brady was right on his heels. "Mama!"

She dropped down to his height and opened her arms, her heart seeming to take a deep breath as her sweet little boy pressed against her. She kissed his hair, smelling his head. He was hers. The most important thing in her life now and forever, and she wondered again if she should find a different career.

But she was in so much debt from Joe's company —

start-up debt that he would've dealt with over time had he lived — she couldn't afford to take a position that paid less than her current one.

They hadn't gotten around to increasing his life insurance since he opened shop—a stupid mistake that made his death that much more difficult to deal with. They'd been so busy, him trying to get the new company up and running before he'd even quit his job at the hospital.

"Brady, baby. I missed you so much. Were you good for Grandma and Grandpa?"

"We played Play-Doh and made forts."

He had chocolate around his mouth, and she dabbed at it with her thumb. "Sounds like fun."

"I missed you." He tucked his head under her chin. "How come you have to work all the time?"

Five years old already. Where had the time gone? She was missing her son growing up and she felt like the worst mother in the world.

It's just because you've been at the hospital so much this week, getting ready for the hurricane. It's not always this bad.

"I don't suppose you got to the grocery store?" asked Theresa.

Touché. If Hannah kept a list of everything she hadn't done to get ready for the hurricane, she'd have one hell of a stack of paper. "We'll be okay."

Teresa shook her head. "You should come with us. There's plenty of room in the RV and it isn't safe for you to stay here."

"I need to be close to the hospital in case they reopen. My place will be fine. It has hurricane glass and everything."

"But the storm surge alone is going to be fifteen feet. You don't understand what that's going to do to the island, Hannah."

"The building is steel. It's more than sound enough to weather the storm, and I can wait out the storm surge as long as I need to. Please, let's not fight about this again." She moved to the table and dug through Brady's bag, looking to see if he had everything. "Where's Mr. Bojangles?"

"In my room," said Brady, who went upstairs to grab his stuffed bear.

Theresa crossed her arms over her chest. "It isn't safe for him to stay here."

"We'll be fine."

"But—"

"Stop." Hannah held up her hand. "Just stop."

Theresa inhaled loudly. The women faced off.

Tom cleared his throat. "We should get a move on."

"I just need to finish up a few things, then we can be on our way," said Theresa. She left the room.

Tom opened his arms and Hannah gratefully stepped into them. "She's just worried about you," he said. "She loves you. You know we both do, honey."

"I know." She pulled back.

"Be safe. Call us if you need anything."

"The phones probably won't be working."

"That's right."

"How far are you going?"

"Up to Richmond. They still don't know which way Oscar's heading, and Theresa doesn't want to have to move again once we get settled."

"Smart."

Brady ran back downstairs. "Guess what, Mom? The weatherman said we might even get a tornado."

She inwardly cringed. "Wow, that's exciting. Say goodbye to Grandma and Grandpa. We've got to get home before the storm comes."

She settled Brady in his booster seat.

"I can do it myself," he complained.

She climbed back into her car, the water falling off her body like she'd just turned off the shower head. She felt better now that he was with her, her shoulders relaxed and her soul much calmer. She could deal with anything as long as she had her son by her side.

Through the rain-slicked glass, she saw her in-laws loading the last of their belongings into the camper.

You should go with them.

The thought caught her off guard.

It would be so easy to change her mind, to gather up Brady and his things and let Theresa and Tom drive them away from this place, leaving the storm behind. It would feel nice to be taken care of, to know she was safe without needing to slay any dragons herself. She wouldn't need to be afraid.

She wouldn't need to be alone.

Her in-laws climbed into the RV and closed the doors, the brake lights shining in her eyes. She started her car.

"I love you, Mama."

"I love you too, sweetie." She backed out of the driveway.

Her condo was seven miles across town back by the hospital and tonight those miles were harrowing. She couldn't remember ever seeing the island so deserted, and she found herself again questioning her decision to stay. It seemed everyone with any sense had left Hilton Head Island in their dust, leaving Hannah and her little son alone to face the storm.

She thought of the tornadoes Brady mentioned and shuddered.

The last thing I need right now is a freaking tornado.

Her shoulders were stiff and tight from driving through

debris when she saw the lights of the corner store where she bought coffee on her way to work. With a grateful sigh she pulled into the parking lot. A big hand-painted sign read NO GAS.

Oh, well. Maybe she'd get lucky and find milk after all.

"Can I get gum?" asked Brady.

He sounded so cheerful, so childish, so unconcerned with the doubts that plagued her, and she loved him so much in that moment she felt her heart might burst. This was fun to him, an adventure, and she decided to do her best to play it off that way. "Sure you can, baby." She unbuckled her seat belt, turning to face him with a smile. "Are you ready to get wet?"

3

Hannah got out of her car with great effort, the wind pushing against it, fighting her, then opened Brady's door for him. In the time it had taken her to get across the island, the winds had gone from bad to worse, and she wondered at the wisdom of taking her son outside, even for a moment.

She held his hand, grateful her parking spot was mere feet from the door of the small store. A bell rang over her head as she went inside and Brady ran straight for the candy section.

"Hi, Dr. Fielding," said a skinny teenage boy, stepping out from behind the counter.

"Hello, Julio. I'm surprised you're still open, though I'm grateful."

"You just made it." He flipped over the sign on the door from open to closed. "My father wanted us to stay open as long as we could, but the news says the storm surge is coming up the beach already. He doesn't want us to get stuck in that."

"That's nice of your father to be concerned with others at a time like this."

"Just like you, *sí*? You stayed in town to help people who need it, right?"

"Yes, I suppose I did. Though the hospital is closed now. I'd like to be here when they reopen." She turned and looked at the shelves, surprised by how empty they were even though she'd been expecting it. "Wow. I guess I'm a little late to the party."

Her eyes connected with a strange man's fierce stare over the empty shelving unit, startling her. Icy gray eyes. Chiseled features. Unshaven with dark hair and stubble covering his cheeks. He was strikingly handsome and a bolt of awareness shot through her body from her head to her toes. She pulled her eyes away.

Holy cow.

Definitely not someone she knew, but that wasn't unusual in this tourist town. She sure as hell would have remembered that face.

"For you, Dr. Fielding, I have milk and bread," said Julio. He walked into the back room.

"Thank you."

She could feel the eyes of the stranger still upon her. "You're a doctor?" the man asked. His voice was gravelly and deep, with a richness that resonated inside her belly.

Working to keep her expression neutral, she met those intense eyes again. "Yes."

"What kind?"

"I'm a surgeon, but most of the surgical cases on the island go to the mainland, except for the stray appendix. That sort of thing. So I do a lot of general stuff."

God, I sound like a moron. General stuff? That's the medical term for it.

A touch of self-loathing made her toes curl in her wet sneakers.

Julio came back with the items. "My father made sure we had plenty for ourselves. We can share with you."

She took them from him with a smile. "Thank you so much."

"Mama, can I get chocolate?" came Brady's voice from deeper in the store.

"No. Just gum."

"Can I get a Spin Pop?"

"If you ask me for one more thing, you're not even going to get the gum."

She glanced back where the man had been, curious to see if he looked at her differently now that he knew she had a kid, but he wasn't there. Disappointment made her shoulders fall. She made her way around the tiny store, conscious of the fact that she was looking for him as much as she was looking for groceries.

She found neither.

She couldn't remember the last time she'd thought a man besides her husband was attractive. What was his story? A renter, perhaps, who didn't heed the evacuation warnings? He was probably here with a woman. A girlfriend or wife. She frowned at the direction her thoughts were taking. She should tell him to leave while he could still get out of town.

A hurricane was on its way, about to terrorize the island with hundred-and-sixty-mile-per-hour winds, and she was flirting with a tourist. She went up and down another aisle, picking up mustard and a jar of pickles just so she'd have something to buy. Anything she might actually want had been snapped up long before.

The bell over the door jingled and she looked up to see the back of the stranger's head as he left.

Figures.

What did you think was going to happen?

He'd ask you out right before the eye wall hit and you'd live happily ever after?

Happily ever after was dead.

She made her way to the counter. "Come on, Brady," she called.

He came running, adding a pack of gum to her purchases.

"I can buckle myself in," he said. "I'm not a little baby anymore."

She shrugged. "Okay, that's fine."

She paid, then they ran through the rain and she opened the door for him, squinting against the wind and pelting rain. She climbed into the front seat and pulled her seat belt on.

"Wow, thanks," said Brady, awe in his voice.

She laughed. "You're welcome." She reached up to adjust her rearview mirror so she could look at him. "Are you all buckled?" Her eyes locked on to the fierce stare of the man from inside the store. She screamed, starting. "What are you doing in here?"

"I'm not going to hurt you," he said.

"He gave me chocolate!" said Brady.

She jumped out of the car and raced to the other side, yanking open the man's door. "Get out of my car."

"I need your help." The man's eyes were beseeching hers. "I have a GSW in my thigh."

Her eyes moved down his body, seeing the tourniquet and bloodstains for the first time. She gasped.

A lot of bloodstains.

"Through and through," said the man, "I can't reach the back of my leg to stitch it up and stop the bleeding."

"My mom's a doctor," said Brady.

She met the man's eyes again. They were no less intense now than they'd been when she first saw them. If she were alone, she would help. But Brady was here and there was a good chance this man was dangerous. "I don't have the supplies," she lied.

"Of course you do. Antiseptic. Sutures. Antibiotics."

He was right on every count. She kept all those things in her medical bag just for emergencies like this one.

No, not like this one. Not like this one at all.

"I don't have any painkillers."

"I don't need any."

The lights of the bodega went out. Any moment now, Julio would be walking out to his car.

"Please," said the man. "Just stitch me up and I'll be on my way."

She didn't move, the storm stinging her skin in her indecision. It wasn't in her nature to refuse help to someone who needed it, but she couldn't put Brady in danger, either. "How did it happen?"

"It was an accident. I was cleaning my gun and didn't realize it was loaded."

Anger was swift. "Don't lie to me. I have every right to leave you on the side of the road."

"I'm begging you, Doc. I've lost a lot of blood. If I don't get help soon..."

She shook her head. He had a bullet wound and he lied to her about how it had gotten there. This man was clearly dangerous. "No. I won't take chances with my son. Now get out of my car."

He nodded slowly. "I understand." He lifted his hands, half covering them with one of Brady's sweatshirts that must have been on the seat. The gleam of metal peeked out at her from its folds and she squinted to make out what it was.

A gun.

He has a gun next to my baby.

Her insides lurched, as if the blood in her veins had come to a screeching halt.

"I'm sorry I have to do this. Take me to your house," he said.

She shook her head frantically. "No."

"I'm trying very hard to make this a pleasant experience for Brady here, but I'm running out of time, Doctor. Now get in the car and drive."

"Take the car. I don't want it. Just give me my boy and it's yours."

"He can't have our car!" said Brady, as if she'd lost her mind.

The man's eyes never left hers. "I don't need a car, I need a doctor. The hospital's already closed."

She didn't move, her feet seemingly rooted to the spot.

"Now," he said.

Her mind was desperate for a different answer, swirling through possibilities that were fruitless and lame. The metallic click of the weapon had her sobbing out loud and running to her door, sliding behind the wheel as she cried.

"Mommy, are you okay?"

"I'm fine." Her voice was strangled and high.

Stop crying, damn it. You're scaring him more than the guy in the backseat.

"Are you sure you don't want some chocolate?" the boy asked.

"I'm sure." She put the car in gear, her feet tentatively touching the pedals.

"Faster," the man said.

The car shot forward, taking them away from the only person who might be able to help her. She was losing control, had already lost it, a line from a self-defense course she'd taken in college echoing in her head.

Never let them take you to the second location.

"Where's your husband?"

"Waiting for us at home—" she blurted, but Brady answered, "In heaven with the angels."

Fuck.

Her son continued, "He died at Christmas when I was four. Santa brought me a teddy bear."

"I'll bet you miss him a lot."

"Are you going to die, too?"

"Nope, your mom's going to fix me right up."

"She couldn't save my dad."

Hannah's heart squeezed so hard it was like a chef trying to wring the last drop of juice from a fruit. She was right back in that moment, Joe on the floor, her performing CPR and pounding on his chest, screaming for him to breathe, *damn it*, when Brady walked in from his room.

It was the worst moment of her life, and he'd shared it with her, right by her side. Her little man had been through so much already in his short life. The last thing he needed was any more trauma.

She squinted into the rain as her headlights caught on the familiar shape of a police car with a truck pulled over on the side of the road. She hit the brakes.

"Keep driving," the man said.

"But there's a policeman. He can help you. He can find you another doctor and you can let us go."

"I said drive."

She continued to slow down, less fearful he would shoot her in front of a cop. Something on the ground caught her attention, though it took her brain a minute to process what she was seeing. A pile of something. A shiny gold reflection. She hit the brake. "What is that?"

"Keep moving, Doctor."

She turned to him, her stare colliding with his just as comprehension hit. Her eyes went wide. "A police officer. On the ground."

"Damn it, go," he snapped.

She was shaking now, her shoulders and her hands and her chest, everything. She turned forward and hit the gas.

"I didn't have a choice," he said.

"That's where you got the bullet wound."

"It was self-defense."

"Stop talking. I don't want to know."

"How much farther to your house?"

"Apartment. A half a mile. Not even."

"Tell me you live on the first floor."

"Third."

He cursed under his breath.

Her mind was racing. The trip from the car to her condo would give her and Brady a chance to escape. This man was badly injured. They should be able to outrun him without much effort.

But what about the gun?

She was still trying to make a sensible plan when she pulled into the parking garage beneath her building. His voice stilled her. "Brady will help me up the stairs, won't you, sport?"

"Sure!" said the boy, clearly eager to be of assistance.

"No," she said, too quickly. "I'll help you if you need it."

His stare was pointed and direct. "I wouldn't want you guys to get too far ahead of me, Doctor."

He was on to her and was going to use her son as collateral. Nausea bubbled uneasily in her stomach. She was powerless, at his mercy, and she wasn't sure he had any.

4

Noah was dizzy from the stairs, fighting for consciousness.

He sat on a kitchen chair in his briefs and a shirt, the lovely Dr. Fielding kneeling beside him and the weather on the living room TV. The hurricane was nearly upon them, winds of almost eighty miles an hour already pummeling the area.

As soon as he'd heard the clerk in the bodega address her by name, his interest was piqued. Not only could she help him, but Dr. Fielding was the same name from the obituary on his sister's fridge. While it was a small world for sure, Hilton Head Island was a hell of a lot smaller than that, and he suspected this woman was the widow he'd read about.

"What's your name?" he asked, struggling to remember from the obituary. Brady was definitely the son's name. Was it Sarah? Anna?

"Dr. Fielding."

"I meant your first name."

"Doctor."

"Her name's Hannah." Brady crossed the room, his eyes fixed on Noah's wound. "Whoa. Does it hurt?"

"A little bit. Not too bad."

"There's scotch," she offered.

"I wouldn't think you'd be inclined to lessen my pain."

"I'm not in the habit of hurting people, no matter what you do for a living." She stood and opened a cabinet, handing him the bottle of liquor.

He opened it and took a long sip. "And what exactly do you think that is?"

"Something illegal and morally reprehensible, I'm sure." She knelt back by his side, opening a small brown bottle. "This is going to hurt."

"Maybe I'm the good guy, fallen on bad circumstances."

"I doubt it." She poured the liquid onto his wound, a pain like the hottest fire searing his nerve endings. He inhaled sharply.

The boy ran away.

"Cute kid," he said.

She glared at him, the exact opposite reaction he'd been hoping to get.

"How old is he?"

"Too young to know he shouldn't let psychopaths with bullet wounds into our car in exchange for a chocolate bar."

Brady returned carrying a worn, stuffed bear. He held it out to Noah. "This is Mr. Bojangles. You can squeeze him when it hurts."

He grinned. "Thanks, man."

Her eyes went from her son to the bear and back again. Brady ran away.

Clearly she didn't like her son fraternizing with the enemy, but God, was she beautiful. Long blonde hair and smart green eyes that held his attention like it was their job. There was a weariness, though, a fatigue he suspected had been there before he climbed into her car.

"You seem tired," he said.

"I'm fine. Thanks for your concern."

"I'm not a bad person, Hannah."

She dug in her medical bag. "Well, you're doing a fairly good impression of one."

"I appreciate what you're doing for me."

Her arms dropped. "You appreciate what I'm doing for you?" she mocked. "You held me at gunpoint and forced me to bring you back here, so don't pretend I'm being nice to you out of the goodness of my heart. I have a limited tolerance for bullshit."

He couldn't help the grin that slid over half his mouth. "I'll try to remember that."

She lifted her chin. "You won't need to. I stitch you up and you go on your merry way. You can even take the car, as long as you drive away in it. Do we have a deal?"

He held out his hand. "Deal."

She nodded curtly instead of shaking it, and he missed the contact he'd been expecting. She was a spitfire, Dr. Fielding, and he found himself wishing they'd met under different circumstances.

The crash of breaking glass made them both jump. "Brady!" She shot to her feet as a cool breeze carrying the scent of the storm made its way to where Noah was sitting.

"The window broke," said the boy, crying as he came into the room.

"Oh my God! Are you hurt?" she asked.

He shook his head. She took his hand and led him away from the outermost wall of the condo. "Come sit by the door."

"Do you have any plywood?" asked Noah. "I can put it up on your windows when you're through."

"I don't need your help." She donned rubber gloves and picked up the suturing needle. "Let's get this over with."

Noah squeezed the bear and took another sip of scotch. He needed a plan. He'd have to take the woman's car— Hannah—no matter that he didn't want to leave her stranded. Chances were good she'd be stuck here for days or weeks anyway, given the flooding that was expected. He ignored the burst of pain shooting up his leg, concentrating instead on the brush of her hair against his knee.

She was the kind of woman he'd normally give his number, not threaten at gunpoint and force back to her place. In his quest for a distraction from the physical sensation of the needle threading his skin, he imagined she was bent over his lap for another reason entirely, those green eyes smoldering before she opened her mouth...

Stop it.

He'd already wronged this lady. She'd be really pissed off if she knew he was thinking about blow jobs.

As if she could hear his thoughts, she looked up at him, her eyes narrowing.

"What?" he asked.

"Nothing." She went back to work.

His eyes went to Brady. The boy didn't seem to understand the situation, which was good. As far as he knew, Noah was a kindly stranger with a boo-boo.

"I can't guarantee this will stop the bleeding," she said. "Sewing up the outside can't fix anything that's torn on the inside, and surgery in my living room isn't an option. But the bleeding isn't bad at the moment. That's a good sign."

"I'll take the best you can do." He clenched his jaw, focusing his mind on what he needed to do now. The sooner he could contact the authorities the better off he'd be, given the circumstances. God only knew what would happen then.

He forced himself not to think about it. "Brady, is your phone working?"

Hannah glared at him. "I told you not to talk to him."

"I was trying not to bother you while you work."

She turned to her son. "Go and see if we have a dial tone. If not, bring me my cell phone from my purse." She went back to work and he closed his eyes. He had to contact Cowboy, too. Would his boss have his back now that the shit hit the fan, or would their earlier argument preclude that?

He was to blame. He could see that now. Hell, he could see it then, but it hadn't made a damn bit of difference.

"No dial tone," said Brady.

The weatherman on TV was on location in Hilton Head Island showing storm surge already reaching ocean-side properties. "How far are we from the beach?" asked Noah.

"Two blocks," she said. Another window broke somewhere in the condo, the needle digging deep into his muscle as she jumped. "Sorry," she said.

He grunted and took another sip of scotch. "Do you have plywood?" he asked again.

"Don't worry about me."

"Answer the question."

She set her mouth. "No."

He shook his head, amazed at her lack of preparedness. "You can't stay here. The storm surge alone is going to swamp this place. It's dangerous."

"The building has solid steel and concrete construction. We'll be all right."

She was kidding herself if she thought that was true. "Maybe if you'd boarded the windows instead of buying mustard. You're not prepared to weather a storm of this magnitude. Do you remember Katrina?"

"I have everything we need."

Now he was getting angry. She had to think about her long-term well-being, and the boy's. "You're exposed to the elements. That's hundred-and-sixty-mile-per-hour winds headed your way, up close and personal. Debris flying through the air. You ever experience anything like that?"

"Don't yell at me."

"I'm not yelling. I'm demonstrating reason and foresight. In addition to the wind, rain, and hail, the building will be flooded and you'll be effectively stranded here. Your car will float away. There will be no electricity and likely no potable water. You have an electric stove and nowhere to make a fire, so no way to purify whatever the hell will be coming out of your tap. How long do you think Brady will be able to make it without clean water?"

"Stop trying to scare me."

"You should be scared. You have a gallon of milk, a loaf of bread, and I'm guessing canned vegetables and beans. Maybe some ramen. Everything in your refrigerator and freezer will rot, and you won't be able to cook any of it anyway. Is that about right?"

Brady brought her cell phone and held it between them, warily. She opened it. "No service. Guess you'll have to wait and call your cronies another time."

"I was going to call the police."

"Why?"

"To turn myself in. I told you it was self-defense. I'm not running away, but don't change the subject. You and your son should go while you still have the chance."

She stood up. "I'm not stupid, you know. I've thought of everything you said long before you said it. But one, I don't have anywhere to go. I'd have to drive hundreds of miles—at least—to find somewhere safe to stay and I'm almost out of gas. You saw the sign at the store. They're sold out, and according to the news so is everybody else. But I have a closet full of bottled water and I don't need to eat. Brady can have it all."

The whites of her eyes were red, as if she was trying not to cry.

"I should have let my in-laws take him but I wanted him with me." She pressed the back of her hand to her mouth for a moment before continuing. "It was a mistake. The windows are supposed to be hurricane glass. They aren't supposed to break..."

She was definitely crying now, silent tears that fell down her cheeks.

"I wanted to leave the hospital sooner," she said. "But I had to get the patients to safety."

"Are we going to be okay?" asked Brady from his corner.

"Of course you are, sport," said Noah. "I'm going to help."

She shook her head. "No. I don't want—"

"You need my help," he said. "Just like I needed yours."

"You don't even have a car."

"I have a pickup truck next to that police officer with fifty gallons of gas in cans in the truck bed. The cop shot out my tires, which is why I was on foot. We can drive your car over there and use the gas."

"No." She crossed her arms over her chest. "We had a deal. I stitched you up, now you need to leave."

"You can't stay here."

She blew out air. "It's a better option than going with you."

"I know how this looks, and I know you're trying to

protect yourself and your son from me." He pulled out his wallet and his military ID. "Noah Ryker, US Navy SEAL Team Four. Now I work for a company out of Atlanta called HERO Force, which stands for Hands-on Engagement and Recognizance Operations." She held the ID in her hands. He could tell from her face she didn't know what to believe. "It's true, Hannah. I'm one of the good guys."

She put her medical supplies away. "Good guys don't shoot policemen."

"I stopped because I thought they needed help. The radio said the cops were already off-duty, but he was there, along with a medical supply truck that was being unloaded. But they must have been doing something illegal because the cop came after me."

"I don't believe that for a second."

"Damn it, come with me."

"No."

He stood and took her by the elbow, her eyes taking in his hand on her before meeting his frustrated stare. "If you stay here, you're putting yourself and the boy in great danger."

"That's my prerogative."

She was fighting with him just for the sake of fighting with him, refusing his help because she believed he was dangerous when really it was her own actions that were threatening her well-being. "Don't make me force you."

"You're threatening me again?" She gestured to his leg. "You wanted me to help you. I've done that. My obligation to you is over."

"Yes, but you saved my life, and my obligation to you has just begun. You're coming with me."

5

Noah stood in Hannah's living room, still in his briefs. He'd given her a few minutes to pack a bag and find him some pants, then they'd head out to his truck to get gas and leave Oscar in their wake.

His plans to mourn Lizzie's death would just have to wait for another time. It was more important these two got to safety and he turn himself in to the authorities.

He wouldn't think too much about the latter right now.

He wandered around the apartment, taking in the photographs and artwork that had clearly been done by Brady. It was a warm space, but he imagined it had been difficult for her since her husband died. One picture in particular caught his eye—Hannah and what could only be her husband with the baby.

Death sucks.

People didn't pass peacefully from one realm into another. They were torn away from those who loved them as surely as if they'd shared the same flesh, leaving terrible wounds in their wake.

He didn't know how he would come to grips with his

sister's death, and he found himself wondering how Hannah had dealt with her husband's.

A plaque on the wall caught his attention.

To Dr. Joseph Fielding, Director of the Hospital Accreditation Team, with our grateful thanks for a job well done.

It was dated a month after he died. He must have been some kind of administrator, completing most of the work before he passed away. Accreditation of any institution was a lengthy process that required every department meet certain standards.

A paper-pushing nightmare.

He continued to walk around the room, arriving at a desk with a corkboard on the wall next to it, the papers on it noticeably yellowed and worn. It didn't take a genius to figure out this was Joseph Fielding's desk and Hannah hadn't touched it since he died.

Noah pulled out the chair and sat down, wondering again who this man was to his sister. Lizzie was an accountant. As the accreditation manager, Fielding would need lots of information from her department. Or hell, maybe he was her direct supervisor.

There was no way to tell for sure.

He wanted to know what their connection was, wanted to understand why Fielding's death had affected his sister enough to keep his obituary on her refrigerator for months on end. If it was an affair, he wanted to know that, too—anything to get some answers why his sweet sister might have ended her life.

If that's what she did.

It didn't sit right with him. It never had.

He pulled open drawer after drawer, rifling unashamedly through the other man's things. He found a wallet-sized picture of Hannah that had clearly been cut out of a larger one, and immediately knew why. She sat by a campfire and looked to be laughing, her beauty leaping from the page, and Noah ran his finger over it before flipping it over.

Love you.

Joe Fielding was a lucky man.

Noah dropped the picture onto the desk and moved to the side drawers, finding one full of files, and he flipped through them, one tab catching his attention.

ACCOUNTING PROBLEMS.

He scanned page after page of documents, including several memos between Lizzie and Fielding as they tried to reconcile the medication inventory with the corresponding paper trail, each time coming up short by thousands of units, the equivalent of hundreds of thousands of dollars' worth of drugs.

The last page in the file was a letter from Fielding to the head hospital administrators making pointed allegations of fraud by someone within the organization. Noah's eyes went to the date. It was less than a week before Fielding died. Handwritten across the top was a note.

BCC: LIZZIE RYKER.

Blind carbon copy. Lizzie had been copied on the letter, but the others didn't know she had been.

"Holy shit."

His mind worked to catch up with what he was learning. Fielding was on the trail of missing drugs and Lizzie knew about it. Noah didn't know how Fielding died, but if there was the slightest possibility Fielding had been killed for this letter...

Then maybe my sister was, too.

He needed to talk to Hannah and find out exactly how

her husband died, and what, if anything, she knew about the alleged fraud at the hospital. But she didn't trust him and he had a limited amount of time with her before he'd be arrested or would have to turn himself in. If he waited too long, there was sure to be a manhunt and his own chances of living would decrease considerably.

He'd have to work quickly.

He was struck by the realization that none of this was random. There was a reason he'd ended up in Hannah Fielding's apartment, one that defied coincidence or simple happenstance. Something had brought her into that bodega at just the right moment for him to find her. He'd come to the island desperate for answers, ready to face the harrowing storm outside.

He glanced to the window and the darkness beyond. Maybe that was exactly what he'd been given.

He gathered the papers into a pile and shoved them into his go bag.

6

Hannah stared at the jagged bits of glass that clung to the frame of her bedroom window, the howling of the wind outside making her feel like Dorothy being lifted by the cyclone.

If she could have shimmied down the side of the building with Brady on her back, she would have done it in a heartbeat, but unfortunately such heroics were a sheer impossibility.

She wasn't sure she believed Noah would hurt her if she refused to come with him, even though he'd pulled a gun on them at the corner store, and she wasn't sure if that made her insightful or ridiculously stupid. The Navy SEAL garbage was probably a line of crap, but she couldn't put her finger on what his real story was. He was certainly built like he was in the military, with legs like tree trunks and arms that could wrestle all day long.

She shook her head to clear it. He was built, all right, and he was desperate. And desperate people did desperate things.

She ought to know.

She'd felt that way for nearly a year now. Joe's death had shattered her world as surely as the storm had broken her window. Where she'd once been strong, she was weak, where she'd once been confident, she was full of self-doubt. Joe had been her rock, anchoring everything she did and even who she considered herself to be. Without him, she was just...drifting.

An odd light shined on the ceiling, and she moved to the window to see what caused it. There, just steps from her building and next to the parking garage, stood a man in the glow of a camera's lights. If he were closer, she could call out to him or signal him in some way, but as it was, he'd never hear her above the roar of the hurricane's winds.

"Mommy, can I bring all my stuffed animals?"

"No, baby. Just Mr. Bojangles, okay?"

"But Bunny and Big Dog are scared of Oscar."

"Okay. Bring Bunny and Big Dog, too."

"I wish Daddy was here."

"Me, too." She turned and stroked his soft little-boy hair. He was everything, the most important person on the face of the earth, and she prayed she'd be able to take good care of him.

There was a knock on the bedroom door. "We need to go now," called Noah.

She looked to Brady. "Go potty." She moved to her dresser and selected a pair of leggings covered in cartoon mice. "One size fits all," she muttered to herself, then opened the door to Noah. "Here."

He cocked his head. "Is that the best you can do?"

"They're very comfortable. You'll never wear anything else, I swear it."

He stepped past her into the bedroom, instantly making her uncomfortable. "Are your husband's clothes still here?"

"No."

He opened the top drawer of Joe's dresser and pulled out a pair of jeans. "What do you call these?"

Her throat was tight. "You can't wear his things."

"I need them."

She snatched the pants out of his hand and stuffed them back in the drawer. "I said no."

"He can't wear them anymore, Hannah. He's gone."

She moved to slap him and he caught her arm in midair. "Fuck you," she ground out quietly. He was so much stronger than her, so much taller and bigger. Everything about him dominated her and there was nothing she could do about that, but damned if she was going to let him hurt her soul, where she was already bruised and bleeding.

"I'm sorry I have to take them, but I do." His eyes held hers as tightly as his big hand clenched her wrist, their steely-gray depths arresting. The air between them was charged, her skin heated at the point of contact, and for a moment she was certain it was hatred in its purest form. But then his gaze slipped slowly down her features, caressing her face with interest so intense she could feel it like a touch, until it landed on her parted lips and she froze.

She couldn't breathe, the moment stretching out between them. She wanted him to kiss her.

What the fuck was the matter with her?

She jerked away from him. "Take the damn pants."

The bathroom door opened, Brady skipping out. "I'm ready."

Noah was standing there as if waiting for her to say something, and she turned her head sharply to the left to avoid him, her eyes going to the picture of her husband she kept on the nightstand. The frame had blown over in the wind, water from outside pooling beneath it, and it was surely ruined—just another blow to her well-being.

She and Brady followed Noah down the stairs, the wind grabbing the metal fire door and slamming it against the building. It was so windy it was difficult to walk outside, Brady unable to move forward despite his hand in hers. Noah picked him up with one arm, leaving Hannah wanting to protest, but Brady was too big for her to carry. It was Noah or no one at all.

Brady smiled at her over Noah's shoulder.

Great. My son's getting attached to a psychopath.

She followed a step behind them through the parking garage. They rounded a dumpster and the TV crew came into view in the distance, lights on and the man out in front of the camera.

This was her chance to get away.

She looked from Noah to the TV crew. Did he still have his weapon within reach or had he put it in his bag? The camera crew was recording. He wouldn't hurt them on TV, would he? If he really was dangerous, she was better off to take her chances now with an audience than to go with him to God knows where.

The parking garage was a veritable wind tunnel but it was headed toward the TV crew. Knowing her voice would carry on the air and echo in the garage, she felt confident a hearty scream would reach them. Uncertainty clawed at her insides.

Don't let this opportunity get away.

She took air deep into her lungs and yelled as loudly as she could. "Help!"

Noah spun around instantly, grabbing her with his free arm. "What are you doing?"

"Help!" she screamed again, as loudly as she could. This

time, the lights changed direction, pointing at the three of them.

"Stop it," said Noah.

"Put down my son." She tried to pull her arm away from him. "They're watching you. They're probably recording this right now."

Brady was holding him tightly. "But I like Noah, Mommy."

"He's a bad man, baby."

Brady frowned and stared at Noah. "Down."

"Just a second," Noah said to the boy, then looked back at Hannah. "Listen to me. My sister worked at the hospital. She was an accountant. Lizzie Ryker. Did you know her?"

Noah was Lizzie Ryker's sister?

There was a resemblance. Those gray eyes that were so intimidating on Noah were striking on Lizzie. And the dark hair. Yes, she could see it now.

She and Lizzie were barely more than acquaintances, but they'd worked at the same hospital for years. "I know the name. She died recently."

"She had your husband's obituary on her refrigerator."

Surprise had her jerking her head back. "I don't understand."

"Neither do I. There's more. In your husband's desk I found a whole folder about discrepancies with the drug supply accounting—"

"You went through my husband's desk?"

"Listen to me! He discovered hundreds of thousands of dollars' worth of drugs missing during the accreditation. He wrote a letter to the head honchos the week before he died, all but pointing the finger at someone in the administration."

Her eyes went wide. Joe hadn't told her that.

But you knew how stressed he was. Something was wrong and he wouldn't tell you what it was.

She figured it was the long hours he was putting in to finalize the accreditation. It was a massive amount of work and he was under a lot of pressure to complete everything on time, on top of all the work he was doing to get his consulting firm up and running.

In her mind she could see him sitting at his desk when she'd gone in search of him in the middle of the night. Her hands had squeezed his shoulders, the muscles tight and knotted, her heart going out to the man she loved, so overworked and tired.

Had there been more to it than that? If Joe really discovered thievery of that magnitude, he'd have been compelled to find the source. That was her husband. Hardworking and honest to a fault, never passing the buck to the next person.

An investigation like that would have put him in danger.

Her throat constricted. In her memory she was clutching the autopsy report, the paper crinkling beneath her fingers, her head throbbing with the need to understand something that defied explanation.

It doesn't make any sense.

The TV crew was only forty feet away, fighting the wind with every step. Their lights pointed at the triad, Noah's face in shadow as he looked back at her.

"How did he die?" Noah demanded.

A pit opened up inside her, threatening to take her down. It was filled with nagging doubt, the kind that reached up when you weren't looking and pulled you beneath the inky surface.

"A heart attack."

"At thirty-four?"

She looked from the news crew to Noah and back again.

You've known for months there was more to his death. Isn't that why the microscope is sitting in your car? Prepared slides of your husband's organs tightly wrapped in plastic inside your purse?

"I don't...I don't know..."

"My sister hated guns," said Noah. "I'm a sniper, for God's sake, but she would never touch one no matter how many times I tried to teach her. They want me to believe she shot herself in the head. There's no way in hell she would do that. Someone else killed her."

Hannah squeezed her eyes shut. What he was suggesting was unthinkable.

"Is it possible your husband's heart attack could have been something else?"

Her lips were trembling. "Joe had a procedure in July to fix a heart murmur. They said his arteries were pristine."

"Not exactly heart attack material." His fingers dug painfully into her arm. "Come with me. We'll find out who did this together."

The camera crew crossed the last of the distance that separated them from Hannah. "Ma'am, are you okay?" a man asked.

She opened her mouth and closed it again.

Am I all right?

7

"Smile," Noah said into her ear.

"Ma'am?" the man asked again. The camera lights were blinding, the force of the wind making her feel like she was standing in the path of an oncoming train.

Noah pulled her against his side like they were a couple. "We're fine, just getting blown away out here," he said. The men's eyes moved to Hannah.

She hesitated.

This was her chance to get away from Noah. She remembered the fear she'd felt when she found him in the backseat of her car. How he'd wrapped a gun inside Brady's sweatshirt and forced her to take him home with her. The dead body of the police officer on the side of the road, for God's sake, and the realization that Noah had killed him.

But she remembered other things, too. Lizzie Ryker at the hospital, always smiling, even laughing at lunch with her coworkers. Hannah had been shocked to learn of her suicide. Noah's version of events almost made more sense.

And she remembered her beloved Joe as she performed CPR, her movements practiced and efficient even as her heart seemed to rip from her body. The autopsy report that added to her confusion instead of settling her mind. The hundreds of nights afterwards when she skirted the abyss of doubt.

This was her chance to find out the truth.

Her stare went to Brady, then Noah, beseeching. Would her baby be safe with this man?

"I'll take good care of him," said Noah. "I promise."

Her mouth opened in shock. How many times had Joe used those exact words? Her husband and his little buddy off on some adventure, a quick wink in her direction.

I'll take good care of him. I promise.

She knew what she had to do.

"Yes, I'm fine. I'm sorry I worried you," she yelled to the men. "The wind is so strong."

She was struck again by how physically fit Noah was, the muscles of his arm and chest wrapping around her body, and she prayed she had made the right decision.

"Do you mind if we ask you a few questions on camera?" asked the man.

"I don't think—" she said.

"Sure," said Noah.

"Why didn't your family heed the mandatory evacuation order?"

She was about to correct his assumption that they were a family when Noah said, "Just go along with it."

She met his eyes, that same steely stare she'd first seen in the corner store that had shot a bolt of longing through her body. She wasn't sure what was happening here, who he was or how his story related to hers, but his question about how her husband died might have been the first honest thing she'd heard in more than a year, vibrating in tune with the piece of her that had known something was terribly wrong.

She would help him now. Play along if need be. She turned toward the camera, a smile on her face. "I'm a physician. I wanted to stay in the area in case I was needed."

"Where are you going?" asked the weatherman.

"Higher ground," said Noah. "You can't be too careful with a storm surge like this one's packing."

The weatherman looked to Brady. "What about you, little guy? Is your daddy taking good care of you?"

A smile burst onto his face. "Yeah."

A little piece of Hannah shriveled up and died. Brady was so desperate for a father he'd clung on to this stranger after a bullet wound and one ride on his shoulders. She must be doing a terrible job as a stand-in dad if that's all it took to replace her.

"How much longer do we have until the worst of it comes on shore?" asked Noah.

"This parking garage is your saving grace at the moment. Out there are sustained winds of eighty miles per hour. I'd say we'll be up to ninety in the next twenty minutes, and into the eye wall where it's currently a hundred and thirty miles per hour."

"Wow," said Hannah.

"Then the eye of the storm after that," he continued. "Maybe half an hour, thirty-five minutes until it will be quiet for a little while, then the other side of the eye wall will hit."

"We'd better be on our way," said Hannah.

They reached the car, Noah putting the boy down and holding out his hand for the keys. It was a small gesture that seemed much more profound. A shift in their relationship. A token of trust.

She put them in his palm and moved to the passenger side, the wind blowing the car in gusts and waves as they drove along the roads she'd driven all her life, things that should have looked familiar now strange and frighteningly new. The hurricane tugged at the landscape, ripping trees from their roots and tossing branches and palms everywhere.

He pulled in behind the pickup truck they'd passed earlier with a cover over the bed and two flat tires, and Hannah made a point not to look at the dead body on the ground.

Noah got out, angling his body against the wind as he made his way in front of the truck. He came back carrying two large gas cans and she popped open the trunk, a strange sort of numbness taking over her mind. It was too much to absorb—all of it. Especially after she'd had so little sleep.

The sudden depth of her returning fatigue seemed to alter her consciousness.

She watched him make several more trips until all the gas cans were stowed away, then he filled her tank. How long had it been since a man had done the hard work while she stayed safely inside? Joe had always done the heavy lifting while she stayed dry—literally and figuratively—and she didn't realize until that moment how exhausted she'd become from doing everything herself.

She was mother and father to Brady, the wage earner, the grocery shopper, the laundry doer, the homework helper, the playmate, the car mechanic, the *every-fucking-thing* doer. And she was so damn tired it hurt.

He climbed back into the car, a wet wind whipping through the vehicle until he slammed the door. "All set."

"Where are we going?" she asked.

"My sister's place. It's not far."

"Is it really on higher ground?"

"No."

"Shouldn't we get away from Oscar like you told the camera crew?"

"I think that ship sailed a while ago. With so much debris on the road and in the air, we're better off just to batten down the hatches and wait out the storm. I have plenty of supplies at her place for all three of us."

"Were you close to your sister?"

"Yeah."

"I'm sorry."

"Thanks. It hasn't had a chance to sink in yet. I got angry when I found out. Mad at the whole damn world. I made some bad choices and probably lost my job."

"HERO Force."

"That's right. I've only been there about six months and I don't think they'll put up with that kind of shit." His eyes went to mirror and Brady. "Sorry. I have to watch my mouth."

"That's okay," said Brady, cheerfully.

"I think you're walking on water right about now," she said quietly.

"I noticed that."

"Sorry. It's been hard for him."

"I like it." He turned to her and smiled, a killer grin that made her insides dance. "Only standing next to a kid can you feel like you're ten feet tall."

"Do you have any?"

"Kids? Nope."

Wife? Girlfriend?

She bit her lip on the inappropriate question.

You're just as bad as Brady.

That was it, wasn't it? She'd been alone for so long her body was reacting to the pheromones in the air. It was basic biology. Human beings' bodies were always looking to reproduce, no matter the circumstance. Probably even more so in the face of danger.

Satisfied with that explanation, her thoughts went back to Noah's sister. "How close in age were you and Lizzie?"

"I was ten when she was born."

"That's quite an age difference."

"That's a built-in babysitter." He laughed. "I didn't mind, though. I liked playing with her. My mom married Lizzie's dad when I was eight. It was just the two of us before that."

"What did she do?"

"She's a therapist. Alive and well and living in Florida with my stepdad. Lizzie's condo actually belongs to them."

His voice was full of love for his family, giving Hannah a glimpse at the side of him beyond what she'd seen so far, and letting her picture what it must be like without Lizzie in their lives.

A lot like my life has been without Joe.

"Do you really think she was killed?"

He was quiet for a moment, so that she didn't know if he was going to answer. "I know I want to believe it. It even seems more likely to me. When I first heard she'd killed herself, all I could think was she's always so happy. Then I heard it was a self-inflicted gunshot wound and that didn't seem possible."

Maybe he was chasing a fantasy.

She didn't say it, but she suspected she didn't need to.

"You're safe with me, Hannah. I'm not going to let anything happen to you or your son."

All the men in the world, and she'd either hitched her

wagon to a cop-killing monster or a military warrior, without a way to know for sure which one he really was.

"I think I have to trust you. I don't have much of a choice."

8

Cowboy was juggling so much shit he must look like a clown in a cow pasture. First Jax decided to leave HERO Force completely, then Noah went off the goddamn deep end and walked off a mission.

He rubbed his new beard, the prickly scruff still feeling strange on his face. He was an understanding guy and he understood Noah had just lost his sister, but Ryker could go fuck himself if he thought he could put personal shit—*any personal shit*—before an active duty mission.

Noah, Stefan, Cowboy, and Booger were five thousand feet in the air over Mexico City when Noah decided to pick a fight, the chopper about to land on the property of a drug lord who had stolen his two American children from their custody-holding mother, a US Marine.

Tensions were running high since Booger had lobbied hard against Noah for an on-foot interception without an active sniper for cover. Booger didn't want the kids to get hurt. Noah didn't want any of the SEALs to die.

"It's fucking bullshit," Noah had said to Cowboy through their headset, knowing full well the others could hear him.

"If that shit-for-brains doesn't think I can tell the difference between a tango and a child, he has no place on this bird or down there on the ground with us."

"We've been over this, Ryker," said Cowboy, who'd already been through this once and had no great desire to go through it again. "You'll cover us from a distance after the initial breach is made."

"The initial breach is what's going to get somebody killed."

"I don't see it that way," said Cowboy.

"You did before this idiot suggested otherwise," said Noah, gesturing to Booger.

Booger crossed his arms and shook his head, otherwise ignoring their conversation.

"He has some good points," said Cowboy, counting on his fingers. "A sniper at the get-go puts the whole house on high alert."

"Oh, because you don't think gun-toting soldiers in fatigues showing up at the door does the same thing?"

Cowboy held out another finger. "And we don't have eyes into the house to see who's answering the door."

"I am capable of visual discrimination. There's the fucking problem. You're acting like I can't be trusted." He jerked his head back. "That's it, isn't it? You don't fucking trust me."

Cowboy didn't look him in the eye, and even as he did it, he knew it was as sure as a giant spray-painted NO on a billboard sign. But there was truth to what Noah was saying. If this was the military, he'd pull another sniper from the bench and sit Noah down on it. The man was a live wire since his sister died, and hell no, Cowboy didn't trust him when two little kids' lives were on the line.

It was that bad.

Hell, he'd almost decided not to take Noah on the mission at all and go without a sniper, but no sniper at all put the men at too great a risk. When Booger suggested an alternative plan that didn't put so many of their eggs in Noah's basket, it seemed like a dream come true.

"Why am I even here?" asked Noah.

Cowboy met his friend's stare. In the time the other man had been with HERO Force, they truly had become that. When Cowboy first learned Noah was a prepper, he'd thought the guy must be off his rocker. Who spent that kind of time and resources to prepare for an event that would probably never come?

So Noah had invited him out to his house in the woods outside of Atlanta. He called it a bunker, and it didn't take Cowboy long to figure out why. What looked like a two-thousand-square-foot ranch was really a steel and cement reinforced structure with a basement twice the size of the house. "I figured as long as I was building it, I may as well build it right," Noah had said.

There were storerooms full of food with what Noah claimed was a shelf-life between five and twenty years, but he took care to rotate the stock. Another room housed his weapon collection with enough ammo to shoot his way through all of Armageddon.

"It's good you didn't put this shit on your resume," said Cowboy.

"Why's that?"

"Because then I would have known you're batshit crazy."

"You ever think about how fragile our supply chain is?"

"Not really."

"A few days' goods. That's all that's kept in our stores today. Everything is on demand. No waste. Food arrives on the shelves when it's needed and not a moment before.

That's why a snowstorm can empty a city of groceries in a matter of hours. There isn't any more in the back beyond a small supply for the next day. What you see is what you get."

Cowboy shrugged. "But they have warehouses full of that shit."

"Not anymore. They used to, sure. But now most of it comes in on trucks and is shipped directly to the stores. Warehousing adds to the cost of the products. It's no longer necessary to keep our shelves full." Noah raised one eyebrow. "Unless..."

"Unless what?"

"Anything disrupted that supply chain. A power outage that affected a large area for an extended period of time."

"Doesn't happen."

"It would if we had an EMP. An electromagnetic pulse would damage all the electronics. It could be naturally occurring from a solar storm on the sun, or it could be deliberately used. Imagine it. Your cell phone wouldn't work. The power in your house wouldn't work. Every appliance broken. Every electronic device down and unable to be repaired. Computers run that supply chain, and the computers wouldn't be working."

Noah walked around the room, touching giant bottles of water one by one as he went. "Then there's bioterrorism. Or natural medical emergencies, like an evolving bird flu or Ebola. History tells us they could strike at any time and knock out society as we know it. Disorder would ensue. Chaos, if you will. The political system relies on a healthy society to keep it functioning. Law enforcement. All of it."

Cowboy narrowed his eyes. "Is this why you became a sniper?"

"It's why I like guns. We need to be able to protect ourselves in any situation. Even the unexpected." He shrugged. "A lot of preppers also prepare to defend themselves against civilians who weren't prepared, those who want their supplies of food, water, weaponry. I prefer to accommodate as many people as possible. So when the shit hits the fan, grab Charlotte and come here. You'll always be welcome."

Trevor walked into Cowboy's office, disturbing his reverie. "I've got a problem."

"Shoot."

He ran his hands through his hair. He looked like shit, which gave Cowboy more pause than anything. Hawk was a pretty boy who always seemed to look good.

"Olivia's got a stalker."

Cowboy leaned forward, tenting his hands on his desk. Olivia and Hawk had been together over a year now, the former SEAL and the movie star an unlikely couple. "In Paris?"

Hawk nodded. "She doesn't want to leave because the movie has another month and a half of filming, which I get, but this guy is starting to freak her—and me—the fuck out. And the security hired by the studio is completely useless. They were watching her while she got a threatening note in her goddamn dressing room and even inside her chauffeured car."

"You want to go to her."

"Yes. But I'm supposed to be here helping you train the new recruits."

"I don't give a shit about them. I give a shit about you." He pointed to the door with his chin. "Go ahead. You have my blessing." Hawk thanked him and left.

Cowboy's cell phone rang. It was Charlotte.

"What's up, hot stuff?" he asked.

"Turn on channel nine."

He grabbed the clicker. Noah's face filled the screen. "... with a storm surge like this one's packing."

The camera moved to a young boy in his arms. "What about you, little guy? Is your daddy taking good care of you?" The kid smiled and looked at Noah adoringly. "Yeah."

"Holy shit," said Cowboy.

"You missed his wife," said Charlotte.

"Noah has a wife?"

"Not as far as I know."

"Who the hell is she?"

"No idea. Some pretty lady. Her hair was wet, but I think it's blonde."

Cowboy had never seen Noah with a woman, much less a wife and kid. "What the fuck is going on?"

"Better question. Why are they standing on the frontline of a hurricane on Hilton Head Island?"

"That's where his sister lived." He could see it, Noah going there after he walked off the job. It was the only place the other man wanted to be.

"Maybe she's just a friend," said Charlotte.

"I don't think I ever claimed a friend was my wife, especially on national TV." The camera followed Noah, the woman, and the kid to a little orange car, Noah climbing into the driver's seat. "The plate number."

"C85 HV9," said Charlotte.

Cowboy wrote it down. "Hilton Head's in South Carolina. Let me see what I can find out about Noah's new mystery wife. I'll call you back." He hung up, immediately dialing Logan. "Wheel yourself in here. I need you to run a plate for me."

9

The microscope.

In their rush to get to safety, Hannah had nearly left it in the car. Given that the vehicle might float away, she needed to bring it inside with them.

It felt like she was carrying the ghost of her husband, an image of Marley's chains popping into her mind unbidden. The expensive lenses symbolized her doubt, her unwillingness to accept Joe's death all these months later, and it weighed her down, heavy in her arms.

The winds were so strong she and Noah had to lock elbows to get from her car into the shelter of Lizzie's condo, Brady wrapped tightly against Noah's chest. Without Noah she knew she'd never be able to walk in this at all, his mass and strength anchoring them to the ground and pulling her forward.

Debris was flying through the air—a stop sign, a bent gutter—so that Hannah finally realized how dangerous the situation really was. She prayed Brady wouldn't be injured as they fought against the wind, barely inching toward the condo doors.

It was Noah who was pulling her, Noah who was taking care of them both. The man had been shot today—for goodness sake—but still he was the strong one leading her tiny family. What would have happened if she was weathering this storm without him?

She shuddered at the thought.

Something blunt and heavy knocked her in the head. She cried out.

"Are you okay?" asked Noah.

The pain was sharp and throbbing. "Yes. Just keep walking."

They reached the front doors, Noah opening one and ushering her inside. Brady looked like a koala bear on his chest, holding on for dear life. He lifted his head, his eyes going wide when he saw his mother. "You're bleeding."

She touched her injury, finding it gooey with more blood than she would have thought possible. "I'm okay."

"I'll stitch it up for you when we get upstairs," said Noah, putting the boy down. "This way."

Hannah followed him to the stairwell, Brady's hand now fisted tightly in her own. Her little boy was dragging, every step taking a Herculean effort from him. It was just past midnight.

She remembered how tired she'd been when she left the hospital, and that was easily four hours ago, maybe more. She was running on fumes and adrenaline. Any moment now she would crash.

Noah had to be exhausted, too. The spot of blood on the back of his thigh showed his wound didn't care for the amount of physical activity he was doing, and she was grateful the finish line was in sight for them all.

"I'm tired, Mommy."

"I know, pumpkin."

Brady clutched her leg while they waited for Noah to find the key. She hoped there would be comfortable sleeping arrangements, but honestly at this point she could sleep standing up with her eyes open.

Hell, maybe she already was.

He pushed open the door to a familiar scene. The windows had broken, tiny cubes of tempered glass covering the floor, curtains blowing violently in the hurricane winds. She squeezed her eyes shut, reminding herself she was lucky to be someplace safe. She shot a sideways glance at Noah. His muscles were bulging from use, sweat light on his brow.

"The worst of the storm is approaching," he said. "We have to hurry. I'll put up the plywood. You sweep and vacuum up the glass."

"I can't believe you still have power," she said.

He smiled, the transformation of his face from frighteningly powerful to sublimely handsome. "Now you jinxed us."

"Right, because if the power goes out in hundred-and-sixty-mile-an-hour winds, it's just because I said that." She turned away from him, more than a little unnerved by her reaction to this man, and settled Brady at the table.

"You're right about the power. I'd vacuum first, if I were you. Then we need to take a look at your cut," he said.

"It's fine."

"You can't even see it." He crossed to her. He was standing in her personal space now, and she bent her head so he could take a look. The angle left her staring at his wet shirt sticking to his muscled chest and abdomen, and she imagined touching him there with eager hands, the heat of his skin seeping into her palms.

Oh my God, I need to go to sleep.

"It doesn't look too deep," he said. "But some stitches would help it stay closed. It can wait, though. I think we should batten down the hatches first, before Oscar walks right in here and sits down, asking for a drink."

"Agreed." She found a vacuum, broom, and dustpan in a closet, glass crunching under her shoes with every step. The task of cleaning up so much spread over such a large area seemed overwhelming in her current state, so she simply went from one task to the next, Brady's favorite Disney movie in her mind as she went.

Just keep swimming.

At one point she looked over and found Brady with his cheek resting on the table, asleep despite Noah hammering up the plywood. She was more than a little jealous.

"You okay?" Noah asked.

"Just tired. I'm sure you are, too. How's your leg?"

"It's all right. Just a little achy."

"I'll take a look at it when we're through."

"And I'll get your room set up next."

"I want to sleep with Brady."

"Sure thing."

She'd gotten in the habit of sleeping in her son's bed after Joe died, and never stopped. There were days where cuddling against his warm little body was the only good thing in her entire world, and while she knew she should stop, she also knew she wasn't going to any time soon.

Noah finished the plywood and moved on to what she hoped was one of at least two bedrooms. She stood in the center of the condo and crossed her arms over her weary chest. When she stood still, she could feel the building moving from side to side—a sickening sensation she tried to put out of her mind. Something heavy flew into the plywood with a crack, making her jump.

"You okay?" he called.

"I think you got that plywood up just in time."

The room went dark, the electric hum of appliances and lights suddenly stopping. The hurricane's winds seemed louder now, swirling around her in every direction, and the hair on her arms stood on end. Footsteps sounded behind her, muffled by the carpet. "I need to find my go bag," he said.

"I think it was by the door." She turned to help him find it. The darkness was complete and she held out her hands in front of her as she walked—straight into Noah. His hands went to her arms. "Sorry," she said, jerking away and changing direction as if she'd been burned. "Over here somewhere."

The sound of a zipper opening several feet away stopped her. "Got it," he said.

"Why do you call it a go bag?"

"Because it's ready to go at a moment's notice, with everything I need." As if to illustrate his point, a small cracking noise preceded the illumination of a blue six-inch stick. "Ta-da."

She couldn't help her smile. "Glow sticks?"

He smiled back. "We prefer to call them ChemLights."

"Either way, Brady's going to be all over those. You'd better hide them."

There was an intimacy in the moment, the two of them grinning in the glow from the ChemLight, and Hannah wondered if extreme sleep deprivation was an aphrodisiac. She was suddenly looking at Noah as a man instead of a threat or a question mark. A big, strong brute of a man who had done more to take care of her in a few hours than anyone else had done in what seemed like forever.

She took a big breath in. "I haven't slept in forty-eight hours."

He stood. "Let's get you settled, then." He handed her the glowing light, cracking another one for himself before scooping Brady up and heading down a hallway.

She followed, the hardworking, masculine scent of him trailing behind him on the air, and she imagined the smell worked like bread crumbs to lead lonely women to love, or at least some mind-blowing sex. A crazed giggle bubbled up from her belly without permission.

"What's so funny?"

"Nothing."

"Must be a really good one if you're not willing to share."

"I'm just tired. Getting punchy."

"Punchy?"

"You know." She shrugged. "Goofy. Silly. Overtired."

He stopped walking and she nearly ran into him, her eyes flicking from the massive wall of his chest and her sleeping son to his eyes.

Sweet Jiminy Cricket.

His eyes were smoldering and for the briefest moment she let herself pretend she might do something about it. "Yeah." Her voice sounded dreamy and suggestive, and she licked her lips, not knowing if she was serious or out of her mind completely.

He gestured to a doorway next to them. "You're in here."

She held up her ChemLight, illuminating the space. There was a king-sized bed, a dresser, a comfortable-looking chair, and a small desk. It was clearly the master. "Where are you going to sleep?"

"There's another bedroom across the hall." He moved to the far side of the bed, pulled the covers back, and tucked the sleeping Brady into bed.

Her fatigue was back, pulling her down like ankle weights in water. She sat on the edge of the bed. "I've got to go to sleep."

"I'll get my suturing supplies."

She wanted to tell him to forget it, that she'd rather just bleed out as long as she could close her eyes, but she just sat there waiting for him to get back, her shoulders slumped forward.

"Hannah, wake up."

Her eyes snapped open. "I'm awake."

"Lean back. I'll stitch it while you sleep."

She blew out air. How could anyone get stitches without waking up? She leaned back on the pillow, unable to stop herself.

The next thing she knew her eyes were closed, the smell of shampoo in the air. A warm, wet cloth gently caressed her head and she moaned softly with pleasure. Noah was washing her hair, cleaning away the blood, and it felt so good to be touched, even like this. She could smell him again, and the scent had the subtle pulse of desire gently beating in her veins.

"You're going to feel the lidocaine," he said quietly.

She furrowed her brow, her eyes still closed. "You didn't have any painkillers."

"I was saving it in case I needed it later."

The piercing of the needle was painful and she was instantly grateful she wouldn't need to feel any more after it. She was fast asleep before he began stitching.

10

Noah closed the door to the guest room, shucked off his jeans, and stepped out of them.

Not my jeans. Hannah's husband's.

He stared at the pile of denim as if it held the answer to a question he couldn't put into words. The wind was howling outside his window, debris hitting the wood like hail, but the hurricane was nothing compared to the storm inside his soul.

What had started as a shitty day in his everyday life had spun on its head and left him battered and worn. If it weren't for Hannah, he didn't know what he'd be like right now.

Hannah.

He sat down on his bed, rubbing the stubble along his cheeks. She was a stranger, not his saving grace. He'd all but kidnapped her, for Christ's sake. He stared into space, feeling the desperation that had coursed through his bloodstream when he'd aimed that gun at her and demanded she help him. If she hadn't, he might not be alive right now, much less aching for her.

And he was aching.

She was so tired she'd all but collapsed into sleep, showing a vulnerability at odds with the way she handled herself during the day. She was strong and determined, bright and outspoken, and he liked her far more than he had any right to like someone he'd treated so badly.

He'd put her in a difficult position, never intending to stay in her company after she'd stitched up his wounds. But once he'd seen how ill-prepared she was to weather the storm, he'd had to step in and force her to take the help she wouldn't accept when he'd offered.

Now she and Brady were under his roof. The poor kid was obviously missing his father and had decided Noah made a suitable replacement. The speed with which Brady adopted Noah made him suspect Hannah hadn't brought any other man into that space since her husband died.

A steady stream of salty air came in through the tiniest space between the wood and window molding, bringing the scent of the storm. They were physically safe here, but having Hannah and her son with him changed things a great deal, lending a wildcard value to the next few days he hadn't been anticipating.

He held the ChemLight to the entry wound on his thigh. The skin around the stitches was slightly inflamed and angry, but it wasn't clear to him if it was infected just yet. He made his way back out to the living room and retrieved his go bag, swallowing a strong dose of antibiotics dry before climbing back into bed.

Hannah had fallen asleep before she'd been able to look at the exit wound, which was just as well since he'd had a hard-on he didn't feel like putting on display.

It had started when she walked into him in the darkness, their bodies connecting and completing the circuit of electricity like a stun gun lighting up the night. The adrenaline that had been pumping through his body all day had primed his system, the idea of sex like a grounding rod for that extra energy, the path of least resistance so difficult to deny.

That was all it was.

He leaned back against the pillows, pulling the fluffy covers over half his body and leaving the other half exposed to the air. He could see her face in the glow of the Chem-Light, so perfect and shining back at him like he'd wished it would all day. Punchy, she'd said. She was tired.

Right.

He would have liked to have woken her up with kisses.

Bad idea, Ryker.

His mind was full of them tonight.

He could have kept his thoughts tightly reined in if she hadn't wanted him, too. He'd washed her hair, her sexy sounds of pleasure almost more than he could bear. It was a good thing the kid was there to rule out any funny business, because the devil on Noah's shoulder wanted to see what other noises he could get her to make—maybe without even waking her up.

Fuck.

He slipped his hand into his briefs and fisted it firmly around his cock, stroking his length while he imagined what he would like to do to her, his mind hearing the sexy sounds she would make when he really turned her on.

There was a knock at the door and he pulled his hand from beneath the covers. "Yes?"

She opened it, the ChemLight once again illuminating her face. "I forgot to check your wound."

"It's okay. I looked at it already."

"The back? You can't even see it."

"I took some antibiotics just to be safe."

She sat on the edge of the bed. "You were bleeding on the way up the stairs. I need to make sure it didn't come open."

"Okay." He rolled onto his side. Instead of going down, his cock was begging for her touch. When her fingers grazed the hair on the back of his leg, he moaned reflexively.

"I think it's infected. What did you take?"

"Eight hundred milligrams of penicillin."

"Hopefully that will take care of it. Roll over."

Fuck. "I already checked the entry wound."

"Would you just let me see?"

He rolled over, his cock tenting the blankets dramatically, the glow of the ChemLight casting heavy shadows. He might as well have been naked.

Her mouth opened into a cupid's bow, her stare firmly on his cock.

"Sorry," he said.

She moved her light closer to his body and pulled back the covers to expose the wound on his other leg, dangerously close to his erection.

"This side isn't as bad," she said, leaning over his leg, and his dick bounced as if trying to get her attention.

Over here!

She pulled the covers back over his thigh. "It's been a long day for both of us," she said. "I think I'll go back to bed."

"Good idea."

She didn't move.

He didn't breathe.

The air between them was as charged as the air outside. She lifted her chin but didn't face him. "I've missed being with a man more than I would have thought possible."

He groaned. "Hannah." Her shoulder was within reach and he touched it, letting her silky skin slide across the pads of his fingers.

He heard her breath catch.

Just from that one touch.

"Come here," he said huskily.

She didn't move. "I'm as bad as my son, latching on to you like this."

"We need each other tonight."

She turned her head, meeting his eyes for the first time, and he saw the desire that filled them, molten hot like lava and desperate for him. She touched his chest, her fingers curling in his chest hair, and he opened his mouth as he exhaled shakily.

She froze for a split second, cursing under her breath before shooting out of bed.

He sat up. "Hannah?"

He heard Brady's small voice calling for her and fell back against the bed. She wasn't coming back. Disappointment gutted him. She'd been right there, as desperate for their connection as he was, her fingers on his skin a tantalizing sensation.

He sighed heavily. It was for the best. Nothing good could possibly come from sleeping with her. She was obviously hurting and admittedly exhausted. If they'd come together, he knew in his heart he'd just be taking further advantage of her, and that sure as hell wasn't right.

No, better he remember why he came here in the first place.

Lizzie.

Yes, he needed to focus. He needed to find out what really happened to his sister. He mentally laid out a plan to learn everything he could about her association with Joe

Fielding and exactly what she'd known. He'd start in her condo, but he'd need to get into the hospital, too.

Which meant the lovely Dr. Fielding would remain essential to his mission, and he would not be letting her go anytime soon. He just needed to keep their relationship on level footing and not give in to the temptation to make love to her before he found out what he needed to know.

11

Hannah awoke with Brady's foot in her face, the boy's body upside down beside her. His limbs were cold and she twisted him around and beneath the covers he was forever kicking aside.

Light spilled through the seam around the window, telling her it was morning. She could still hear the wind outside but it was far better than it had been when she fell asleep. She squeezed her eyes shut as she remembered touching Noah's bare chest, the springy hair on her fingertips and the warmth of his very male, very alive skin.

"Oh, God," she whispered, horrified.

I all but begged him to have sex with me.

Thank God Brady woke up before you straddled Noah like a saddle.

She shook her head. How the hell was she going to face him this morning?

She wondered how bad it was outside. Maybe she could mumble her thanks and skate out the door without further incident. Convinced that was how this would go, she unwound herself from her son and tiptoed from the room.

It was dark in the hall and living room, as well, the windows boarded up with no lights or power. She moved to the sliding glass doors, where a bit of light escaped around the handle, trying to see outside. The doors were the only glass still intact in the condo.

"I'll take the plywood off of there for you," said Noah.

She spun around. "I didn't see you there."

He stood. "I've been up for a while."

"What time is it?"

"Just past ten."

He went down the hall, returning with a hammer. He walked like a panther and her throat felt dry. He pried the plywood away from the sliders. He was shirtless and wore pajama pants, the muscles of his back and arms standing out in relief from the shadows.

Sex appeal on a stick. That's what he was. She shook her head to clear it. "Do you have anything to drink?"

"Bottled water in the kitchen. When I get this open, I can make coffee. The camp stove needs to be outside."

"I'm not a coffee drinker. I like tea."

"You're welcome to look in the cabinets. Lizzie might have had some tea."

She moved to the kitchen and found the water, taking a long sip before exploring the cabinets. It felt wrong to be going through the cupboards of a woman she barely knew, who'd died right here in this very place. Teacups, plates. Glasses. Was Noah right? Had Joe shared his concerns about the missing drugs with Lizzie Ryker?

A tall cupboard proved to be a pantry, a small selection of tea bags on the top shelf. She walked back into the living room, the doors now uncovered, a stunning view of the ocean beyond. Noah opened the door and stepped onto the balcony, wind whipping into the condo. She followed.

"Look down. We're like an island," said Noah.

She moved to the railing. Where there should have been a beach, there was only water. It continued to the condominium, where it splashed against it like the sea on cliffs. She gasped. "How far do you think it goes?"

"I already tried to make it to street level. There's water in the stairwell about half a flight deep—maybe six or seven feet. From the hallway window on the second floor all I can see is water."

"Wow."

"Yeah."

They stood quietly for several minutes, her thoughts wandering to last night. She would have slept with him. Just like that, mere hours after he pointed a gun at her, she would have climbed into his bed like there was nothing to it but a little no-holds-barred lust. What the hell was wrong with her?

"Hannah, about last night..."

She sucked in her stomach. She was embarrassed and more than a little disgusted with herself, and her cheeks heated. "It was a mistake. I know."

"That's not what I was going to say."

She dared a look at him, those damnable steely eyes homing in on hers. "Can we just forget it ever happened?" she asked.

He looked out at the ocean. "We're going to be together for days. You don't want to talk about it?"

"What is there to say? *Sorry I threw myself at you last night, it won't happen again?* I feel stupid enough already without that conversation."

"Why do you feel stupid?"

She rolled her eyes. "Oh, please."

"We both wanted the same thing. I don't feel stupid. Out

of line, for sure. I took advantage of you yesterday—first when I needed your help and later when I brought you to this place when you didn't want to come. It was wrong of me to think of you that way, but there's no reason you should feel anything but desirable."

His words made her body light up, warmth curling in her midsection.

"I just wanted to apologize," he said. "I won't cross that line again."

She folded her arms over her chest and stared at the ocean. Just how long were they going to be here together? She'd never lived through a hurricane and had no idea how long it took the waters to recede.

One night with this man and she'd already behaved badly. The very last thing on earth she wanted to do was have a repeat performance of last night, and the longer they were together, the more likely that was to happen.

"When Brady wakes up, I'm going to go through Lizzie's desk and see what I can find, just like I went through your husband's. I'm going to use this time to find out what I can, but after that, you should know I'm going to ask for your help one last time."

"What now?"

"I need to get into the hospital."

"No. I can't do that."

"She's my sister. I have to do everything I can to find out what happened to her. Don't you want to know if Joe's death was really a heart attack or not?"

She swallowed her reluctance to share the depth of her suspicions. "The microscope. I brought it home from the hospital along with some slides I had prepared from his body at my own expense."

"Why?"

"I told you I had my doubts about his cause of death." She shrugged. "I'm a doctor. This is how I investigate."

He nodded. "We both need answers. You can set up on the dining room table if you like."

"Thank you."

"I am going to need your help to get into the hospital, Hannah."

"Even if I let you in the front door, the offices are locked. There's nothing I can do to get you inside them."

"I can get past a lock. Is there an alarm system?"

"Some of the doors are alarmed. Not all. I'm not sure how much of the building will be powered by the backup generators."

"Probably just the ones I want to get through. That's usually the way it works." He gave her a sardonic grin.

She moved to the microscope and carried it to the table. "Brady could sleep through a three-ring circus. You don't need to wait for him to wake up if you want to get started."

"No time like the present." Noah left the room.

She lifted the plastic cover off the microscope, running her finger down its arm. "No time like the present," she whispered. Her eyes stung as she moved to get the slides out of her purse.

12

"Her name is Hannah Fielding. She's a doctor of surgery for Hilton Head Hospital. Widowed late last year when her husband—also Dr. Fielding—had a heart attack at the ripe old age of thirty-four. She has one child, Brady, who's five. Husband had just opened a financial consulting firm at the time of his death but was still employed by the same hospital." Logan put down the paper he'd been holding. "That's all I found on her."

"Her husband was a busy guy," said Cowboy. "Maybe the stress led to the heart attack. Any connection to Noah?"

"Nothing, though Noah told me his sister worked at a hospital. Maybe Lizzie was a mutual friend."

"Very possible, though it doesn't explain why they're masquerading as husband and wife. You don't think they could actually be married?"

"I don't see how," said Logan. "No records to that effect."

"Right. Stupid idea." Cowboy tipped his chair back, balancing on the back two legs. "So it's strange, but other than that, we don't have anything to be worried about."

"There's something else."

Cowboy lowered his head and looked at Logan as if over a pair of invisible glasses.

Logan frowned. "The Hilton Head Sheriff's Department is missing one of their officers. Deputy Jerome Buchanan disappeared just as the storm was coming on land. The last license he ran through the system was Noah's. Hilton Head PD has issued an APB."

"Son of a bitch." Cowboy slammed his chair down. "So he goes to the island and gets pulled over. The cop goes missing and Noah shows up being interviewed by a weatherman with his make-believe doctor wife and son. What in the hell is going on over there?"

13

The only way to make sure Noah didn't miss anything was to go through the entire file drawer. Lucky for him, his sister had been organized to a fault. Everything was clearly labeled, every folder containing exactly what it should. There were appliance warranties she wouldn't need and vacation brochures for trips she'd never take.

It was fucking horrible.

There was a file labeled MEMENTOS filled with photographs and ticket stubs and he knew he couldn't look at them right now, so he pulled it out and placed it on the desk for another time—a time when he could wallow in it for a while.

Bills. Insurance. Copies of medical claims. The usual crap everyone kept in file cabinets, but no smoking gun. He went through the desk drawers and, when that proved fruitless as well, moved on to her dresser and nightstand. The condoms beside the bed gave him pause, though of course they shouldn't have. Lizzie was only a child in his mind, not in reality.

He couldn't help but wonder who she'd been seeing. She'd never confided in him about a boyfriend, recently or ever. He always assumed she kept that stuff to herself, and that was just fine with him.

That's when he found the diary tucked into the night-stand on the opposite side of the bed. He put it on top of the MEMENTOS file while he finished his search, but almost an hour later, he'd found nothing else of significance. He grabbed the diary and file and made his way back out to the living area.

Hannah was leaning over the microscope intently, her pose reminding him she was a doctor—a professional woman with a quick mind—and it struck him he normally didn't date women like her. He stuck to the ones with low-cut blouses and names that ended in *i*. Maybe he should change that, because Hannah's brain was damn near as sexy as her body.

Or maybe it's just Hannah you like.

"How's it going?" he asked.

"I'm not sure." She leaned back. "Nothing's making sense. There are crystals on the kidneys and lungs, as well as parts of the cardiac tissue itself."

"What does that mean?"

"If he were being treated for unusual potassium levels or a chemically induced arrhythmia, those findings would be perfectly normal. But he wasn't."

"So what else can cause that?"

"I don't know. I need to do some research. How did you make out?"

"I found her diary. I have to read it. And some pictures and other things she saved."

She got a faraway look in her eye. "I remember when Joe

died, the hardest things for me to go through were the stupid little bits of his life that never mattered. A Post-it note where he'd scribbled 'buy lightbulbs.' That sort of thing. I was finding them for months. It seemed like he'd just stepped into the other room and he'd be back again in a minute, which of course he never was, and it would hurt all over again."

"I came here to Hilton Head so maybe I could feel something." He hadn't intended to tell her what was in his heart, but it was just there, the obvious response to her confiding in him. "Since Lizzie died, I haven't been able to do that. I've just kept it all inside like I was waiting to find out it had all been a terrible mistake and she was really okay. I fucked up my job, alienated my boss. And you've got to understand, the job is everything to me."

"I'm sorry."

He didn't know why he was telling her these things, but he couldn't seem to stop. "I got here yesterday and all I wanted to do was get drunk. I was headed to that bodega looking for beer so I could get smashed and scream at God for taking my sister."

She stood and moved to him, opening her arms. He was holding himself rigid, as if he were a physical dam keeping his feelings at bay. He tried to warn her with his eyes not to come too close, that he might break and everything would come crashing to the ground.

He lifted his chin. "Don't."

"But I—"

"Don't." He moved into the kitchen, silently cursing himself for his weakness. He didn't know if he was afraid he was going to cry or afraid he would kiss the living sense out of her, either one of which was reason enough to back the fuck away. He opened a cabinet and stared into it, unseeing. "I'll make us something to eat," he called.

"I'm not hungry." She walked past the kitchen and into the bedroom, closing the door behind her.

14

Noah scrambled eggs on the balcony over a camp stove. They were in the fridge, still good, and he thought of Hannah's comment about Post-it notes. A simple thing like the eggs being fresh enough to eat was the opposite of comforting. His sister had just been in this world.

Now she was gone.

He'd spent the last hour and a half reading Lizzie's journal. While he did find out who she was dating—her boss in the accounting department at the hospital, Eric Manning—he didn't find anything suspicious or otherwise interesting, and he wanted to get into her office at Hilton Head Hospital even more.

He looked down at the water, the level now halfway up a window it had previously covered. He had the inflatable boat he'd taken from HERO Force, but if he headed for the hospital, Hannah and Brady would need to come with him, and he wasn't sure it was the best idea to take the boy out in these conditions.

"Hi."

He turned to find Brady standing in the doorway, wide-eyed from sleep. "Hey, buddy. Are you hungry?"

The boy nodded.

"Is your mom awake?"

"No."

He imagined her curled up beneath the covers. "Just you and me, then." He scraped the eggs onto a plate, passing it to the boy. "You sleep okay?"

Brady nodded.

"What grade are you in?"

"I'm not in a grade."

Noah narrowed his eyes. "Kindergarten?"

"Mmm-hmm."

"You get to take a bus?"

"Yep." He took a bite of eggs and spoke with his mouth full. "Do you have a dog?"

"No. I travel a lot for work." *Or at least I used to.*

"My dad said we could get a dog. We just had to convince my mom."

"Convince her, huh?"

"That means make her think she wants a dog, too."

Noah smiled. "What kind of dog would you get?"

"A big one. It would play fetch with me and sleep in my bed every night."

He cracked more eggs into the tiny pan. "Do you know how to swim?"

"Uh-huh. I'm a minnow."

"A minnow?"

"I used to be a polliwog. Now I'm a minnow."

He nodded, understanding. "Swimming lessons."

"Mmm-hmm."

Hannah appeared in the doorway. "Tell me you're not going swimming in this mess."

Her cheeks were flushed from sleep, her skin creased between her breasts. "Boating. I'll have to rig a life vest for Brady."

"You're kidding."

"We need to get inside the hospital."

"And you just happen to have a boat?"

He smiled. "Actually, I do."

"Why?"

"I was headed to a condo on the beach in the middle of a hurricane. It seemed prudent to bring a boat."

"Who does that?"

"I do, and look, we need it."

She crossed her arms. "I still don't think it's a good idea."

He finished cooking the eggs, handing her the plate when he was done. "Come inside. I want to show you what I found."

She was eating, which was good, no matter she was less than enthused about the first step in his mission to find out what happened to his sister. He pulled out the stack of papers he'd taken from Joe's desk, spreading them out on the dining room table and selecting the one he'd read at her house that was addressed to the administration. "Read this."

She sank into a chair and put down her eggs, taking the letter from his hand. Noah sorted the other papers into piles by what they were.

"He never told me any of this," she said. "Why wouldn't he tell me?"

"Maybe he wanted his suspicions confirmed before he shared them with you."

"We told each other everything. Or at least I thought we did."

"All couples have their secrets."

She flipped through papers. "What else did he keep from me?"

"All of these are accounting discrepancies he encountered during the accreditation."

She picked up a wallet-sized picture of herself, staring at it before her eyes met his accusingly. "Where did you get this?"

"In the desk. Top drawer."

"It was Joe's favorite picture of me. He always kept it near him."

"I'm sorry. I was looking at it and it must have gotten mixed in with the papers."

"It wasn't yours to take." She shook her head. "I'm grateful to you, Noah. You helped us shelter against the storm. I wasn't prepared and you were."

"I hear a but coming."

"But all the rest of it needs to stop."

He thought of her sitting on the edge of his bed in the night, his body's reaction to her, and how badly he'd wanted to do something about it. "That's fine."

She gestured to Brady on the balcony. "And you need to stop ingratiating yourself with him."

"I didn't encourage that."

"You didn't discourage it, either. It's been hard enough for him losing a father. He doesn't need to get attached to you just so you can disappear in a few days."

He set his jaw. She was blaming him for what was happening between them, the nagging attraction that begged him to act. But she was also blaming him for Brady's reaction to him. "I won't be mean to him because it suits you. He's a good kid. I like him."

"If you like him, you'll spare him the pain of growing attached to you."

"Are you sure we're talking about Brady here, Hannah?" She glared at him.

"The picture is what upset you," he said. "And it has nothing to do with your son. I think you like that I took your picture, that I wanted to look at it, and that scares the bejeezus out of you."

She stood abruptly. "I don't want him going across the island in a boat."

"That's fine, but the longer it takes us to get into that hospital, the longer you and I will be stuck together. Are you sure you want to wait for the water to recede on its own?"

He had her between a rock and a hard place all over again, and he watched her thoughts play out on her beautiful features. He wanted to be angry with her, but what he felt for her—protectiveness, admiration, lust—was a far cry from anger.

"Go without me. I'll give you the codes and the keys. You don't need me there."

"You know the players. You know the layout of the offices and building. It's not just the access you can provide."

She rolled her eyes. "Fine. We'll go today. The sooner we can get away from each other, the better."

15

Hannah was hot, the life jacket around her torso making her hotter. The sun was beating down onto the black inflatable boat they were sitting in, sun that belonged on a beach on a tropical island instead of a disaster area flooded with foul-smelling water. A dark line of purple clouds hovered on the horizon promising even more storms, and she didn't know which was worse.

She focused on the light breeze that kissed her sweating face as Noah navigated the debris-filled lake that now covered Hilton Head Island. "Take a left after the post office," she called out to be heard over the motor. Noah had a map, of course—*was there anything that man didn't have?*—but for now she was telling him how to get to the hospital, her everyday commute looking like a foreign apocalyptic land.

They rounded a corner, another boat coming into view. This one was bright yellow and its sole occupant eyed them through binoculars, making Hannah uneasy.

"Leave the talking to me," said Noah.

She didn't like him telling her what to do, as if her words

could be a liability, but she didn't fight him on it, either. As they got closer she recognized the man from television. He was the local sheriff, Mike Bogardus.

"Afternoon, neighbors," said the sheriff. "What are y'all doing out here this fine day in July?"

"Just surveying the damage," said Noah. "There's a lot of destruction."

"There certainly is. Were you two aware of the emergency evacuation mandate for Hilton Head Island issued by the governor?"

"We are," said Noah. "We chose to weather the storm from our home."

She bristled at his implication that they lived together.

"And how did you make out?" asked the sheriff.

"Just fine," said Noah. "Some broken glass. That sort of thing. Nothing we couldn't prepare for. How about you?"

"Fine, fine. You wouldn't happen to have some identification, would you?"

"Of course, officer." Noah handed it to him. "Is there a problem?"

The officer stared at the license. "One of my men went missing before the storm hit. Deputy Buchanan. The last contact he had with the station was a traffic stop out on 278 just as the storm was about to hit. Some guy named Noah Ryker from Atlanta. Former Navy SEAL. He may be dangerous."

Noah hadn't given him his actual ID at all. Her eyes latched onto Brady's, silently telling him to keep his mouth shut.

The sheriff handed the license back to Noah. "If you see Buchanan, please let him know I'm looking for him. Thanks for your cooperation, Mr. Greene."

So Noah had given him a fake driver's license. Her heart

was skipping in her chest. Who carried something like that with them? For a split second she found herself torn. Should she tell the officer that this was Noah Ryker, and go with the officer instead?

Nothing's changed. He has a fake ID on him. That's all.

And he thought to give it to the officer, choosing to hide his real identity.

That wasn't all he had, however. He had a boat and guns and a map. He said he liked to be prepared for any eventuality, but what if he really had an agenda, plans of his own that were not what he claimed they were?

"We'll definitely keep an eye out," said Noah.

The sheriff nodded. "Be safe."

The boat moved forward. "You said you were going to turn yourself in," she whispered.

"I need to find out the truth first."

She narrowed her eyes. "If they find out what happened to Buchanan, they'll come after you first and apologize later."

"No. They won't apologize at all."

Noah glided smoothly away.

16

Hannah walked down the eerily dim hallway of the building where she'd spent the majority of her time for the past three years. The air was normally filled with the sounds of monitors beeping, patients and staff chatting, elevators chiming as they arrived on the floor, but today there was only the sound of their footsteps and Brady whining.

"I'm hungry."

"I know, baby. I'll get you a snack soon."

Noah touched her arm. "I have a protein bar in my bag."

She snickered. "Of course you do. Go ahead and give it to him."

"You want one?" he asked.

"I'm good. My office is right up here." She needed to get her key ring with the fob that would give her access to the rest of the hospital. "Hopefully the fob is working with the emergency generator on."

"I think it will be. They had to have accounted for staff movement throughout the building in an emergency."

She stopped at her office door, surprised to find it ajar.

She looked to Noah and he held up his hand, drawing his weapon before gesturing for her to move aside with Brady. He opened the door with his foot. "Nobody's in here," he said.

"But somebody has been. I know I locked that door before I left. I always do." She pushed past him into her office. Papers were scattered over her desk and a large portion of the floor. "What the hell?"

"You said a bad word," said Brady.

"Heck. What the heck? Who would go through my things?" She bent and gathered papers from the floor, Noah helping her pick them up.

"What's in here?" he asked.

"Personal correspondence. Administrative paperwork. Things like that."

"Someone who thought you might know about the drug theft. When's the last time you were here?"

"Yesterday, though it feels like a year. I went right from the hospital to my in-laws, then the corner store where you found me. But that doesn't make any sense. Joe's been gone almost a year. Why would they think I knew something now?"

Noah frowned. "Something must have changed. How many people were left in the hospital when you were here?"

"It's hard to say, exactly. A few, but it's a big building. I certainly couldn't see them all."

He handed her his stack of papers and they stood. "I thought you weren't a coffee drinker," he said, gesturing to a mug on her desk.

"I'm not." She picked it up, her eyes going wide. "This is still warm."

He withdrew his weapon again. "Is there anywhere secure I can take you and Brady?"

"Anyone with access to my office has access to ninety-nine percent of the hospital."

"What about the other one percent?"

"The isolation ward. It requires a PIN. Only a few people have it for security purposes to prevent the spread of contagious disease."

"Let's go."

"Wait, let me grab my fob. And my computer."

"Why do you need your computer?"

"I need to research the slides from the autopsy."

"They won't have Internet access."

"We're probably the only place in all of Hilton Head that does. Satellite link. Necessary for emergency patient care."

"We need to be quiet, Brady," Noah said. "Can you do that for me? No talking at all?" The boy nodded.

They walked quickly and quietly, Noah leading the way as Hannah directed him up two flights to the isolation ward. She entered her code and the keypad lit up green as the mechanical lock disengaged.

It was dark inside. "Don't turn on any lights, even if they work," said Noah. "You need to be safe without anyone knowing you're in here."

"What about you?" she asked.

"I need a plan and a map of how to execute it. We'll use the bathroom and a ChemLight to see." The three of them sat on the tiled bathroom floor. Noah produced a small notebook and Hannah got to work on a map of the hospital.

"I'm scared," said Brady.

"Come here, sport," said Noah, opening his arms to the boy, who climbed on his lap. Noah looked to Hannah. "Is this okay?"

"Given the circumstances, yes." She drew a long rectangle with a central hallway. "On most floors, these are patient care rooms. But on the second floor they're administrative offices. Here's accounting, where your sister worked."

"Where's the head of her department?"

"Right here," she said, pointing to an attached corner office. Her pen moved across the hall. "Here's the hospital director's office, and his secretary." She moved the pen down. "HR. A conference room."

"Are there any administrators on any other floors?"

"No, just this one. Who are you looking at?"

"Lizzie was dating her boss, the head of the accounting department, Eric Manning. I want to check him out. Would he have keys to your office?"

"No."

"I didn't think so." He pointed to the largest office, which belonged to the hospital director, remembering the name from the letter in Hannah's husband's desk. "This guy. Thomas Patel."

She licked her lips. What he was suggesting was preposterous, yet undeniably likely at this point. "Be careful."

"Be careful," Brady parroted, giving Noah a big hug.

When Noah extricated himself, he unzipped his go bag and withdrew several items, tucking them into the pockets of his pants before he turned to Hannah. "Whatever happens, stay in this room. If I don't come back within an hour, use the Internet to contact anyone you can and let the authorities know you need help. Under no circumstances should you come out alone."

She nodded. "If you're right, these people have a lot to lose. Be safe."

"I will."

"And I'm sorry for what I said to you earlier." She looked at her hands. "I was upset with myself."

He touched her cheek. "You shouldn't be." He leaned in

and kissed her softly on the mouth. "There's nothing wrong with this."

She was as stunned by her reaction to his words and kiss as she was that he'd spoken them and done it at all. She simply nodded, taking it in stride rather than rallying against the feelings inside her.

Brady took her hand.

"Lock the door behind me," said Noah.

And he was gone.

17

The emergency lighting blinked intermittently, giving the hallway a fun-house look that was anything but enjoyable. Noah made his way through the hospital, weapon drawn, aware of every door he passed and the unknown that might be tucked away inside it.

His money was on Patel for the bad guy. The administrator had access to Hannah's office and motive coming out his eyeballs. Either he was in on the scam to steal nearly half a million dollars in drugs from the hospital or he was complacent in something else. The buck stopped with him, at the very least, though Noah thought he was likely far more culpable than that.

He made his way into a stairwell, brighter than the hallway before it, and arrived on the second floor. He checked his sister's office first. The door was locked, and he wondered if it had been since she died, dismissing the idea as unlikely. Hell, maybe they'd already hired her replacement and he was about to go through the filing cabinet of new employee number three hundred and six.

He used a hairpin and the multi-tool from his pocket to pick the lock, letting himself inside. Lightning flashed outside the window, illuminating an angry purple sky, and he marveled at the quick change in the weather.

Another storm is the least of your worries.

He moved behind the desk, trying each of the drawers and picking the lock on the only one that wouldn't open. This was definitely his sister's desk, with matching blue office supplies, a document scanner at a perfect forty-five-degree angle, and a puppy desk calendar, and for a moment he missed her so acutely he thought he might scream.

He closed his eyes and took several deliberate breaths before moving to a tall file cabinet.

The drawers weren't even full, with just a few hanging file folders full of requisition forms, time-off requests, and mailing labels. He cursed under his breath. If he was going to get into Lizzie's records, he'd have to get into her computer account. Would it have access to the emergency generators? He started up the machine, the quiet hum of the fan surprising him. Billing was apparently a very important hospital function.

He shook his head, a password screen popping up to greet him.

BUTTERCUP.

Lizzie's beloved dog who died right before Lizzie graduated from college. He hit enter, smiling when the machine continued booting up. She was predictable, that was for sure.

His eyes went back to the document scanner. Given that the file cabinet was empty, she must scan all of her papers into the computer—including the letter she received from Joe Fielding. A quick browse through her file structure and he found the scanning program along with its associated images. Again his sister's love for organization proved supremely helpful. He found the letter filed under PERSONAL & CONFIDENTIAL.

It was identical to the one at Hannah's house, except this one had a handwritten note scrawled across the top. It read, "Now they'll have to answer me." Joe Fielding, no doubt referring to the administrators he believed were involved in the missing drugs. He narrowed his eyes. Lizzie's boss and lover, Eric Manning, was one of those addressed in the letter.

He thought of Hannah's earlier comment when she read the letter Joe had written.

Why didn't he tell me?

He always tells me everything.

Wasn't that what lovers did? Spouses and significant others? If Lizzie's boyfriend was involved and he knew she was aware of the letter, he would be under a great deal of pressure to keep her quiet. Joe Fielding had died without pointing a finger or even blowing the whistle on the drug scheme.

"Lizzie was the only one left who knew," he whispered.

A noise in the hallway made his head snap up. Footsteps. Had Hannah come looking for him though he'd told her not to, or was someone else in the building?

You already know someone else is here.

Hannah's open office door and the warm cup of coffee proved that.

Another office lay beyond Lizzie's like an old-time supervisor's to a secretary's, the door open. Noah moved into it, drawing his weapon as he moved behind a tall plant and flattened his body against the wall. He left the door open as he'd found it and waited.

He heard a key in the lock of Lizzie's office door and it

opened, heavy breathing like the intruder had run hard. The chair squeaked and rolled. "What the fuck?" said a man's voice.

Noah winced. He'd left the computer on.

"Who's in here?" the man asked.

The chair rolled again, more slowly this time. Noah trained his weapon at the open doorway of the inner office. The distant sound of someone running reached his ears. Was someone else coming to join the intruder or had the intruder taken off?

He moved to the doorway, training his weapon at Lizzie's desk chair. It was empty. He ran to the hallway, straining his ears to hear as he went in pursuit, his legs pumping beneath him as he ran. He rounded a corner just as the man went through a doorway at the other end of the hall.

Noah was fast, his body well-trained. The doorway was a stairwell and he pushed through it, ready to take a shot if he needed to, but finding the stairwell empty. They were on the second floor. According to Hannah's information, there were patient rooms upstairs and a flooded first floor below them.

He climbed the stairs two at a time, reaching the third of four floors.

The bastard could be anywhere.

He pushed out onto the third floor and withdrew a small CS gas gun from his pants pocket and settled it in his left hand, keeping his Glock in his right. He shot a canister of tear gas into the stairwell behind him and closed the door, assuring the tango wouldn't be able to use it to escape.

One by one, he cleared each hospital room. A terrific thunderstorm now raged outside the windows, his search punctuated by bright flashes of lightning and loud, booming thunder. Most of the rooms were classic doubles with the privacy curtains pulled back. He checked under the beds and in the bathroom and moved on.

Then he got to a big room. It was far larger, several of the privacy curtains pulled. Noah shot a tear gas cartridge into the room, went into the hall, and waited, his Glock trained on the exit.

No one came out.

He cleared the rest of the rooms quickly and entered the second stairwell at the opposite end of the building. He emerged onto the fourth floor and checked rooms, again arriving at one that was larger than the others. He shot tear gas into the room and waited.

The door opened and a man came flying out, clutching his eyes and coughing.

"Freeze!" said Noah, but the man ran past him toward the clear stairwell Noah had just used. Noah fired into the man's leg and he fell to the ground, quickly scrambling up again. "Freeze!" he yelled again.

This son of a bitch is going to make me kill him.

He shot for the man's legs again, missing him completely as the tango ran. If he was willing to take a shot at the man's torso, he would make it, but the shot could be lethal and Noah wasn't prepared to lose this man and whatever he might know about Lizzie's death.

He hesitated.

The man pushed into the stairwell at the opposite side of the hospital. This time Noah was on him, close enough to hear his footfalls, the fresh blood on the concrete like a well-marked trail. They were going up again, one final steel door opening onto the roof.

The man was running full speed toward the edge.

"Stop!" yelled Noah.

The man skidded to a stop as if obeying him and backed

up to the knee wall surrounding the rooftop. He held up a hand toward Noah, now just fifteen feet away. "Don't come any closer or I'll jump!" the man said, squinting, his eyes red and crying.

Noah froze, raising his hands toward the angry sky. The wind on the rooftop was whipping at his body and he feared the other man would be blown right off the edge. "Be careful of the wind," he called out.

The man laughed. "You shot me in the leg, now you don't want me to get hurt? Who are you, anyway?"

"Lizzie Ryker's brother."

The man's eyes went wide. He put one foot on the knee wall.

"What are you doing?" Noah demanded.

He put the other foot on the knee wall, his arms extended at his sides as he came to a stand. "I loved her. I want you to know that."

That's when Noah recognized him. This man was at Lizzie's funeral, had stayed to himself, crying in a corner. "Eric Manning."

"I wanted to marry her."

"But you killed her instead."

His eyes were pleading. "No! They wanted me to, but I couldn't."

Noah's finger twitched on his gun. "You were stealing drugs from the hospital."

"No. I didn't do that."

"You did."

"I looked the other way. I was paid not to pay attention."

"You killed my sister."

"No! I loved her."

"Who did it, then?"

Manning looked over the edge and Noah thought he was

going to lose him. The slightest movement would send him falling to his death.

"Tell me who!" Noah bellowed.

At that moment, lightning struck the HVAC unit on the rooftop with a sound like a freight train hitting the ground. Sparks flew everywhere, Noah reflexively covering his head and jerking away. Time slowed so it was barely moving at all, his mouth forming the word *no* as he watched Manning lose his balance and fall from the knee wall.

Noah ran to the side, another flash of lightning illuminating the body as it rose to the top of the water below.

18

H annah sat in a hospital bed, Brady curled up against her side. She stroked his silky hair, her eyes trained on the storm beyond the window as she worried over Noah and what was taking him so long to return.

Please let him be safe.

She was weary from this hurricane, tired of the weather that threatened the island and turned everything into a scene of destruction and fear. She longed for sunny days and warm breezes, for the life she used to have, filled with the people she loved and the sense that they were blessed. Lucky.

She certainly didn't feel lucky now.

She felt forgotten, as if the whole world had fallen to pieces around her—she, Noah, and Brady the sole survivors.

And whoever the hell is inside this hospital.

She told herself not to worry, that Noah was a Navy SEAL who could take care of himself, but now that she knew her husband's death was deliberate, no one's safety seemed assured.

Her laptop was sitting on the tray table nearby, closed. She'd found what she'd been looking for. All the strange findings from Joe's organ slides could be attributed to administration of the same compound. She felt certain her husband had been poisoned with a drug called atryptoglycol that destroyed certain sensitive tissues before triggering full cardiac arrest.

Her beloved Joe had been murdered.

Further toxicology tests on the blood samples in the pathology lab would confirm her suspicions, but in her heart she knew she'd finally found the answer she'd needed for so long. She sat in the dark, thinking about her son, who would forever grow up without a father despite the depth of her husband's love for Brady.

Sometimes life wasn't fair.

And what about you?

She let herself feel the self-pity she usually kept at arm's length. She'd lost so much, too. The love of her life, the only man she ever wanted to be with. Her mind conjured an image of Noah unbidden, and she admitted to herself that she wanted him physically.

It wasn't love. Her feelings for the dark and dangerous Navy SEAL had nothing in common with what she'd felt for her husband, but he certainly managed to rouse the aching emptiness in the pit of her stomach.

The part of her that needed a man to feel alive.

The thunder rolled and she let herself imagine she could take what she wanted from him, no strings attached. A single night to indulge her body with another, to feel his hands on her skin—so desperate for his touch.

Would he be a considerate lover? She frowned. Would the experience be the balm she needed for her soul, or would it chafe against her battered heart? It was a terrible idea, but how she wanted to make love again, to share that kind of intimacy with another.

She'd never been one for casual sex, never allowed a man into her bed outside of a committed relationship, but she'd already shared so much with Noah it seemed like they were at least as close as some of the earlier lovers in her life.

What are you doing?

She closed her eyes and inhaled her son's scent, grounding herself back in reality.

Noah would be out of her life in a day or two—tops— and she would go back to being just a lonely widow without anyone to look at her like he did with those smoldering gray eyes.

A knock at the door had her and Brady sitting up straight. "Stay here," she said, sliding off the bed and heading for the door.

"Hannah, let me in."

She exhaled a breath she hadn't known she was holding and unlocked the door. The tension coming off him was palpable. "What happened?" she asked.

"Eric Manning is dead. He fell off the roof. Maybe he jumped. I don't fucking know."

"Oh my God..."

"He admitted to his involvement in the drug theft, but he claimed he only looked the other way and allowed it to go on."

"Then who's in charge of it?"

"He died before he could answer that." He dropped into a squat and opened his arms. "It's okay, buddy. Come here."

Brady went into his arms. She watched Noah's strong arms wrap around her son, saw him stroke Brady's hair and back. Instead of being angry or upset, she was surprised to realize she wanted his arms around her, too. She hugged herself. When Noah stood, Brady put his head on Noah's hip and hugged his leg.

"We should head back to the condo," Noah said. "There's no point in staying here and I don't feel I can properly secure the area like I can back at Lizzie's."

"What about the storm?"

"We'll be okay. It's the lesser of two evils right now. How'd you make out with your research?"

"I think I found it. A chemical compound that causes all of the damage I documented, culminating in cardiac arrest."

"So they were both killed."

She nodded. "You were right."

"I'm sorry, Hannah."

She shrugged, fighting off an unexpected wave of emotion. "I'm sorry, too. Not that it does a damn bit of good, unfortunately. They're still gone and we're still here without them."

He opened his arm to her. She hesitated, then leaned into him. The muscular column of his neck smelled masculine and sharp, stress and adrenaline clearly present in this man. His arm was around her back, just as she'd wished it would be, and a jolt of sexual awareness ran through her body.

She leaned back. His eyes were focused on hers, his gaze intense, and she knew she was not the only one who felt it. She was conscious of Brady watching her. "We should go," she said. "Let me get my computer."

The flush of sexual arousal heated her cheeks, the room air cool against them as she crossed the room. She wasn't entirely sure what was happening between them, but it felt good. Too good.

If she had any sense, she'd stay away from this man, but all she could think about was what might have happened if they'd been alone.

19

Noah turned off the icy water, his body cold but clean.

Let's be honest. A cold shower was just what you needed.

They were back at Lizzie's condo. Hannah insisted on making them something to eat so he could clean himself up, and he jumped at the chance to put some space between them. Ever since he'd gotten back to the isolation ward at the hospital, his dick had the distinct impression he and the lovely Dr. Fielding were going to get it on.

He remembered how he'd opened his arms to her, the softness of her body as she fitted herself against him and held on. He forced his thoughts away from her. If he wasn't careful, that shower was going to be for nothing.

He thought of what he'd learned today.

He wished the phones were working so he could call his parents and tell them their daughter hadn't killed herself, hadn't wanted to leave this earth. It was small consolation but a consolation nonetheless, and they deserved to hear it as soon as possible.

Wrapping the towel around his hips, he headed for the bedroom. The smell of something savory filled the hallway, the distinctive glow of candlelight illuminating the space. There was a cozy feel of home, all of his needs being addressed, and again he thought of laying Hannah down and making love to her.

Was it possible she wanted the same thing? Was that why he couldn't shake it?

He dressed and returned to the living room. Brady played with cards in front of a candle, Hannah on the balcony cooking. He sat down with the boy. "You know how to play War?"

They were halfway through the deck, Brady winning, when she came back inside. "I hope you don't mind, I opened a bottle of wine," she said. "Would you like some?"

"That would be great."

She brought him a glass of red, the spicy woodsmoke flavor of the wine matching the ambiance in the room perfectly. They ate pasta with red sauce and played Go Fish, finishing the bottle of wine.

Noah couldn't remember the last time he'd enjoyed an evening more.

Hannah put Brady to bed, and he wondered if she would return, and what would happen if she did. Her eyes had danced all through dinner and the game, joking with him playfully every step of the way. She was flirting with him, and he was flirting back.

God, was he flirting back.

He paced the living room. The wine had made him relax, even made him think it was possible she would come to him tonight, and he hoped more than he ought to hope he was right.

When she entered the room, she met his stare.

"I wasn't sure you'd come back," he said, his voice low and gravelly.

"I wasn't sure I should. But I wanted to."

He moved to her, every step a tactical decision in a game he wanted desperately to win. He stood in front of her, her head tilted up to face him, her cheeks flushed.

He kissed her, her lips soft and welcoming beneath his, slightly open. Blood rushed to his cock. She tasted like wine, with a lingering sweetness that made him think of dessert. She was perfect, meeting his kisses with her own, fitting her body against his growing hardness.

His fingers skated up her arm and into the hair at her nape. "I want to make love to you," he said.

He didn't think he could bear it if they weren't on the same page, if she didn't want the same depth of feeling from him that he needed from her. Better to get it all out there so she could strike him down in one fell swoop rather than make him believe she wanted him.

"Me, too." She went up on her tiptoes and kissed him, her hands settling on his shoulders like they'd been there a thousand times before.

He squeezed her and picked her up, carrying her to the sofa and setting her on his lap as he kissed her. She was softness and curves, her body rounded and satisfying beneath his eager hands. She shifted so she was straddling him, holding his cheeks in her hands before kissing him tenderly.

Provocatively.

Lustfully.

As she deepened the kiss, she moved against him, and they might have been making love already if they hadn't been fully clothed. He wrapped his arms around her hips, pulling her tightly to him as his mouth made its way down her neck. She smelled like cinnamon and tasted like salt, the combination decadent and exciting.

He ran his hands inside her shirt and over the skin of her back, pressing his chin and mouth into the fullness of her breasts, kissing her through the fabric.

She lifted the hem and pulled the shirt over her head, exposing her bra, and he pulled one cup down beneath her nipple so he could see her. "You're beautiful," he whispered reverently, lapping at her nipple before sucking it into his mouth.

"Fuck," she whispered, and he smiled, moving to the other breast and showing it the same attention.

Her hands fisted in the material of his shirt, pulling at it. "Take this off," she said, helping him pull it over his head and kneading the muscles of his shoulders. "You're so big and strong." Her hips pitched on his, rocking back and forth. "Does this hurt your wound?"

"No. It's lower."

"Good. You're so fucking hot," she said against his mouth, then kissed him passionately.

He'd feared she wouldn't share her body with him, yet she was riding him wildly, proudly squeezing his hand on her breast as she writhed against him. He was in awe of her sexuality, her brazen desperation to connect with him, and he wanted to take control of her like she was taking control of him.

In one strong movement he flipped her onto the couch, holding her against it as he settled between her legs with his full weight. He took over their kisses, demanding she meet his rhythm and punishing her with his hips, loving the way she panted in his ear and threw her head back against the cushions. "I need to get a condom out of the bedroom," he ground out against her mouth. "I won't wake Brady."

"He's in the guest room. I thought we might want the big bed tonight."

He pulled her to a stand, loving her plan and eager to take her up on her offer. She followed him to the master bedroom, her hand wrapped tightly in his, and he turned on her when they got there, quickly unfastening her bra and stripping her of her pants and underwear.

She closed the door. "My turn." She unzipped his fly and freed his throbbing cock, which instantly grew bigger, begging for her touch. She pushed him back on the bed and followed him down, taking his length in her hand and nuzzling his balls with her face, her warm breath on his ball sac.

"Oh, God," he bit out, anticipating her hot, wet mouth on him before she took him in, licking and sucking until he was almost completely inside. His hand slipped into her hair, holding her to him, and she took the last two inches of his cock, the head of it now firmly nestled in her throat, suction nearly making him come undone.

She lifted her head. "Where are the condoms?"

"The nightstand drawer."

She took one out and sheathed him, then climbed on top and guided him into her body. She sank down slowly, crying out as his length disappeared inside her, rocking onto his cock.

"Jesus," he whispered. "Just like that."

She moved on him, arching her back. He grabbed her breasts in his eager hands, loving the feel of her body milking his with every stroke. He needed to make it as good for her as she was for him, needed to fuck her hard and fast, get as deep inside her as he could be when she came tightly around him.

He flipped her on the bed, forcing her body to accommodate his size, the pulsating walls of her tight channel telling him she was already on her way to orgasm. Her body clenched his cock again and again, her hips angling up to meet his, and she cried out.

He kept thrusting against her fisted muscles, his body beyond stopping the orgasm, his balls lifting higher as he came with a mighty roar. He fell on top of her and rolled onto his back, taking her with him, their bodies still intimately joined and their breathing coming in heavy pants.

His fingers lightly stroked her heated back, a thin film of sweat making his skin drag against hers. He kissed the top of her head.

Hannah.

The sensible part of his brain knew their time together was limited, that this relationship that had started at gunpoint would never survive once the hurricane moved out and life on Hilton Head returned to normal. But another part of him clutched at her, not wanting to listen. Tonight he'd gotten a glimpse of what their life together could look like and he didn't want to give it back, didn't want to give it up before it ever really got started.

His mind was drifting, fatigue pulling at him. He could see Brady's face lighting up as they played cards, knew there was an answering smile on his own features. He didn't want to give it up. Not the woman, not the family or the warm glow that had covered him up tonight like the warmest blanket.

What are you saying?

She sighed contentedly and kissed his chest, snuggling closer.

Even if he wanted to stay with her, he'd killed a police officer. His very freedom was in jeopardy, the choice to stay or go completely out of his hands. All he could do was make the most out of the time they had together.

He moved his head, rubbing his cheek against her hair. He could smell her shampoo, and he grinned at the familiar scent. This time with her was precious, and he wouldn't waste a moment of it worrying over what was to come.

He fell into a deep, sated sleep.

20

Hannah felt Noah's breathing even out, his abdomen rising and falling steadily with each breath, and knew he was asleep. It occurred to her she should feel sorry but she didn't. If anything, she wanted him again.

He had a cock that women's fantasies were made of, thick and long and hard, the tip bulbous and fat. Even the taste of him had fueled her desire to have him, her quest for satisfaction leading only to a greater need, and she decided to let him sleep for a while to get his strength back before she went after him again.

She'd gone nearly a year without sex and knew she might go longer without it the next time, so she had every intention of fucking Noah until his energy and his balls ran dry.

Hell, I might even fuck him some more after that.

She needed this to remind her she was human after so many nights as an aching mass of grief. Joe was gone but she was alive, and living people needed to be touched and loved, to come together and pleasure each other.

I need it.

She held no illusions about this man. If the ocean weren't flowing beneath this building, he'd be long gone from here. But he was here now, present as any person could be for another, and she was going to take full advantage of the situation.

She moved out of his arms, separating their bodies and rolling him onto his side, amused when he didn't wake up. He was tired, and for a moment she felt guilty for what she was about to do—the very furthest thing from letting him sleep.

Her hands stroked his back, glorying in the deep moan of pleasure that resonated in his chest. She kissed his skin, then stroked him again. She repeated the same motions on his neck and upper arms. Massage, then kiss, with strong hands and an eager mouth as she made her way around his body.

She slipped down lower on the bed, moving to his calves, then his thighs, the springy hair she'd first touched when checking on his bullet wound. He had one leg curled in front of the other, leaving his inner thigh exposed, and she slipped her hand between his legs to tease him.

His breathing was heavier now.

She raked his ass cheek with her fingernails, making him gasp. She kissed him there, her hand coming around his hips to gently squeeze his balls, promising more to come if he was willing.

He moved so quickly he startled her, grabbing her by the arms and hauling her to the other side of his body. He latched on to her breast, taking her nipple deep in his mouth, and she smiled wickedly.

His mouth went lower, skating over her abdomen and into her soft curls. She lifted her knees and he bent his head, kissing her most intimate places and pleasuring her with his tongue. She'd never felt anything like it, the way he moved against her giving her more pleasure than she'd ever gotten from a man. Frenzied noises came from her mouth, sounds she didn't recognize as her own, then his fingers were inside her and she came apart in his hands.

She'd barely come back to earth when he commanded, "Get on your hands and knees." She flipped her weakened body over, doing as he asked. He thrust into her with one hard push, his wide member filling her swollen sex like he was made to do so. She bent her arms, no longer strong enough to hold herself up, resting her head on the pillow as he drilled into her from behind, the slap of his balls on her clitoris a steady rhythm that had her coming to a crescendo once more.

The speed of his thrusts increased. He bent over her body and took a breast in each of his hands, pumping into her while he squeezed her nipples.

A fierce orgasm ripped through her body, pulling her consciousness apart, and he pumped into her harder and faster until he found his own pleasure. They collapsed onto the bed in a sweaty tangled heap, his cock still tightly stuffed inside her, and this time it was Hannah who was quickly carried away to sleep, her body and her mind well and thoroughly exhausted.

21

Noah wasn't sure what woke him. He stared into the darkness, listening, but all he could hear was breathing.

Hannah.

Images of them making love filled his mind. She was incredible, so daring and bold, taking what she wanted and reveling in the sexual experience just as he did. They were equal partners in bed, the first time he'd ever been with a woman he could say that about, and he wanted to do it again.

He rolled over intending to do just that, when he opened his eyes and found Brady sleeping between them.

No more sex for you, tonight.

Suddenly feeling all too naked, he sat up, finding his briefs and pants on the floor and pulling them onto his body before lying back down. The room was dimly lit by moonlight and he stared at the two of them—Hannah and Brady. The boy's presence changed his dynamic with Hannah, almost forcing him into a father-like role, and he was all too aware of how that could be misinterpreted by Brady.

Kids didn't understand the transient nature of certain adult relationships.

Hell, I don't understand it myself.

Because it wasn't just messing with Brady's mind to have the three of them snuggled here like one happy family, it was messing with Noah's mind, too.

You've got to stay focused.

He wasn't here on some kind of romantic mission. He was here to find out what had happened to his sister and he still hadn't done that. His mind replayed the scene with Manning on the hospital roof and he wished he'd had the chance to interrogate the other man and find out what he knew before he died.

He was all but out of options.

A loud thud had Noah sitting upright in bed.

What the hell was that?

He was out of bed in an instant, slipping to the floor and moving to the door like a ninja in the night. He grabbed his firearm as he made his way into the hallway, another loud thump clearly coming from the door of the condo.

He went back and woke Hannah, shaking her shoulder. "Someone's trying to break in."

She was groggy. "What?"

"Someone's trying to break into the condo. Lock the bedroom door," he said. "Stay here with Brady."

"Oh my God!"

He ran to the other room just in time to see the door bust open as if it had been propelled by great force, two men in black with ski masks entering the space. Noah fired twice into both men and they each went down but quickly got back on their feet.

They were wearing body armor.

Holy fuck.

He had the ammo to deal with it, Kevlar-piercing rounds that could go right through bulletproof plates, but they weren't his default ammo and sure as shit were not in his gun.

Only head shots would save him now.

He thought of Hannah and Brady in the next room. He had a hell of a lot worth saving, and he thanked his lucky stars he was a sniper. Two more bullets had the two tangos down, this time permanently. Blood and brain matter were splattered in dark splotches on the wall around the doorway, but men kept coming and Noah kept firing.

The men fired, too, and Noah knew he might be hit. Adrenaline was a funny thing, blocking out all sorts of wounds at the time of impact. Time was his saving grace. His attackers had just as much time to kill him as he had to kill them, and Noah was faster.

He was counting bullets, a habit that had kept him alive more than once. The magazine held fifteen rounds. He'd reloaded after his run-in with the cop on the side of the road, another habit that had served him well. So far, he'd put thirteen into these black-clad intruders.

Fourteen.

One shot left.

Three more men came at him.

How many of these guys were there?

He fired at the first, killing him instantly, then Noah lifted his leg in a roundhouse kick that caught the second man off guard before he could fire his weapon. The third held his gun trained on Noah's head. "Freeze, motherfucker."

Noah put his arms in the air, one of the men coming around behind him and securing his wrists with zip ties.

The one with the gun came closer. "Where are they?"

"Who?"

The man behind him punched him in the kidney. "Dr. Fielding and her kid. They weren't at their place, so we figured they're here."

"No."

The one with the gun snickered. "You check the bedrooms. Mr. Ryker and I will wait here."

Noah hoped they'd hidden, hoped against hope they could avoid being found, but he worked to keep his concern from showing. He narrowed his eyes. "You sure know a lot of stuff."

"Like your name? You gave that to the police officer you killed when you handed him your license."

"How do you know about that?"

"We went looking for him when he didn't show up as expected."

"And this condo," said Noah. "How did you find me?"

"How many Rykers do you think there are on this island? The first one that came to mind was Lizzie. Some coincidence, I was just here a few weeks ago. Standing just like this."

Every color in the room seemed to converge to a single point in the middle of the man's ski mask. "You killed her," Noah said.

The man laughed. Noah forced himself to notice details. Eyes so brown they were nearly black. The man's frame and build. His hands and skin tone. His height. His shoes. He was considerably taller than the other man, nearly as tall as he. This was his sister's killer, standing not more than five feet away, and if Noah got away, he sure as fuck needed to know who to go after.

"I did. That was messy, though I see you took out the carpeting." He cocked his head at the condo walls. "Not this messy, but still. I imagine it was difficult."

The other man's voice came from behind Noah, and he twisted around to see him. "I can't find the kid, but I got the doctor." Sure enough, he held Hannah's elbow, her wrists clearly bound behind her back, as well. She wore a short nightgown and he was glad she'd also dressed before being dragged out here like this.

"Where's the boy?" asked the man with the gun.

"With my in-laws. They evacuated for the hurricane."

"All right, then. Let's get a move on."

"Where are we going?" she asked.

"To the roof. I figured you should die the way you killed my brother."

That piece of information clicked into place, tying everything together in Noah's mind. "Manning was your brother, and you killed Lizzie? He was in love with her."

"That's why he pussied out. Somebody had to do it. Now let's go."

It was hot in the stairwell, the smell of rot and water ubiquitous in the air around them. Noah trudged up the stairs, his mind strategizing his escape. He had several options, but Hannah complicated every one, so he took his time, deliberately making the men slow down so he could think.

Lizzie's condo was on the second floor of a four-floor building, and they were nearing the top. He met Hannah's eyes just as the group rounded the final landing before the roof access. She was scared, he could see that. But if he wasn't mistaken, she also looked pissed off, and he found himself admiring her spirit in the face of intense stress.

It was possible they were both going to die, being marched up these stairs like the damned to the gallows.

Not if I have anything to say about it.

The lead man reached the door, a heavy metal lock hanging from a chain securing it closed. He cursed and stamped his foot.

"Shoot it, dumb ass," said the other man.

The first did as he was told, the blast echoing off the

concrete walls of the stairwell like an explosion. The door opened to the orange rays of the sunrise streaming over the horizon.

But there was something else—the faint thump-thump-thump of helicopter rotors in the distance. Noah glanced at the men, wondering if they recognized it or if it would need to get closer before they realized there was a chopper nearby. It was probably a news crew or a disaster relief effort of some kind, but Noah added signaling them to the top of his list of options.

They just needed to stay alive long enough to do it.

"Sit down, Hannah," Noah said.

She turned to look at him and dropped to the ground. So did he.

"Get the fuck up," said the taller of the two men.

"Why can't we just shoot them here?" asked the other.

"No. I want them to feel the fear Eric felt, to know what it's like to see that muddy water rushing up to meet you, the concrete right beneath. They will suffer for what they did."

The sound of the chopper was closer now, and the men noticed. "What the fuck is that?" asked the shorter one.

"Probably just the goddamn Weather Channel," said the other.

The rays of sun hit the side of the chopper and Noah saw the dark green color for the first time. His eyes shot to Hannah's, then back at the chopper. That was no weather station. It wasn't first responders, either. That chopper was military, and it was heading right for them.

Hope lit in his breast that it might be HERO Force, though he didn't know how they could have found him. But there were two armed tangos on the roof and it was high time Noah gave them a run for their money.

He got up on one knee. "Let's get this show on the road,"

he growled, coming to a stand. He bent at the waist, lifting his zip-tied hands high over the back of his head, then slammed the loop made by his arms and conjoined hands over his buttocks. The zip ties snapped, and in one continuous movement he grabbed a knife from his tactical pants and straightened, elbow bent. He whipped the knife at the shorter man, the gun falling from the tango's hand as he was struck just above his heart.

The taller man pulled his gun, training it on Noah. "You son of a bitch," he said. "What are you, some kind of killing machine?"

The chopper had finally gotten close enough now to rouse the tango's alarm, and he turned around to see it, raising his gun at it.

The red HERO Force logo was clearly visible on the side.

Noah swiftly moved behind him and twisted his neck, breaking it with a practiced yank, the crack of bones loud enough to be heard over the chopper. He let go and the man fell to the ground.

He moved back to Hannah, cutting through her zip ties with a second knife from his pants.

"How many knives do you have in there?"

"This is my last one." He pulled her to a stand. "We have to get out of the way so they can land."

"Land?"

They moved to the stairwell entrance and the chopper descended, landing in the middle of the roof like a leaf falling to the ground. Noah yelled to be heard over the noise. "HERO Force."

"The men you work for?"

He nodded. The sound of the rotors slowly died down. "Stay low," he said, moving toward the helicopter. Her hand on his arm stopped him.

"I have to get Brady."

"I'll go with you. Hang on." He jogged to Cowboy and Booger, coming out of the cabin. "How the fuck did you know I was here?"

"Little interview you did with your wife on TV." Cowboy pointed to Hannah with her chin. "Who is she?"

"Hannah Fielding. A doctor. She saved my life. Come on, I'll introduce you, then we need to go find my son. He's still downstairs."

"Your son?" asked Booger.

"Not mine, hers. That's what I said."

He didn't see the look the men exchanged behind his back as he moved back to Hannah, anxious to get downstairs.

23

Hannah sat near Noah in the helicopter, Brady tucked between them. The boy had been inconsolable after she pulled him from behind the dryer, where she'd hidden him just seconds before the man in black came bounding through the door.

He'd heard the gunshots and feared she was dead, and that reality crushed her heart. She wouldn't be able to take that memory from him. She could only pray it would become less pronounced with time.

Like the memory of his dad dying on the carpet?

She swallowed the bitter taste in her mouth. Thank God he'd stayed put and hadn't seen the blood that covered the living room. She'd shielded his eyes with her hands on their way past.

There was nothing she could do to make any of this better except hold her son tightly and kiss his sweet head, telling him it would all be okay. He seemed to be sleeping now, and she was grateful for that.

The helicopter pitched and Brady squeezed her hand more tightly. Not sleeping, then. He'd taken hold of her hand in one of his and Noah's in the other when they'd gotten on board, the moment too tender for her to object or even apologize to Noah for Brady's behavior. There was simply the little boy she loved, clinging to the people who were pivotal in his safety.

She couldn't even allow herself to consider what could have happened if things hadn't gone their way. Losing Joe had been difficult, but losing Brady was unimaginable.

Her eyes wandered around the cabin. The chopper was enormous inside, far bigger than she would have thought from looking at it, but she wasn't much for flying and sincerely hoped they'd make it to Atlanta soon.

And where exactly do you think you're going to stay?

She hated relying on the kindness of strangers, but that was what she'd have to do. She hoped Noah would take them in for the night, but she knew they were likely to need shelter far longer than he might want to provide it.

Atlanta was only four hours' drive from Hilton Head, and the hotels were likely to be full of evacuees. But it didn't matter now—she'd stay anywhere if she had to—they were alive and everything else would sort itself out somehow.

She snuck a glance at Noah, his stubbled face now inching closer to an actual beard. Was he happy their time together was coming to an end, or was he reluctant for them to part, like she was?

Don't be clingy.

It was sex, that's all. Not even a date or anything that might imply even a temporary commitment. They'd been caught up in the storm and the situation and had done something they would never have done under ordinary circumstances.

Bullshit, Hannah. You would have slept with that man any time.

But would she have? Was he really that attractive, that interesting to her, or was it just the stress and heat of the moment that had captivated her? She and Joe had dated for years before getting married, but she'd known he was the one for her an hour after meeting him.

She didn't trust her ability to tell right now.

In that moment she wanted so desperately to go home, back to her apartment and the safety she imagined she'd find there, but it was an illusion. Her haven was gone, the building flooded and the windows shattered. God only knows what had happened to it since she left. She felt untethered, as if without that apartment she had no idea where to go or how to provide for her family.

Her son.

It was just the two of them, and she'd do well to remember that.

24

Noah sat at the HERO Force conference table, his hands at his sides, dangling toward the floor. There wasn't a single part of his soul that remained untouched over the last forty-eight hours, from his love for his family and the safety of a child to lust and feelings for a woman he had no right to be feeling right now.

He leaned his head back and stared at the recessed light over his head, the intense beam overwhelming his retina. Lizzie was still gone, but he now knew who'd killed her, had snuffed out the life of that man as surely as that man had done to her.

I'm not done.

I need to find Joe's killer.

Even as the helicopter had taken them back to Atlanta, he knew he would need to return. His vengeance would not be complete without giving Hannah the same vindication he was experiencing now, not to mention her safety.

The men in black had known her address, had been to her condo before coming to his. They knew where she lived.

And while those men were dead and gone, Noah knew there was someone higher up who had ordered her death, just as they had ordered his own. Hannah didn't know the men had been to her place and he wasn't about to tell her.

Cowboy walked into the room and sat down heavily at the head. "Drink?"

"I'll take a water."

Cowboy opened a small fridge and put a bottle in front of him. "You doing okay?"

"Nope."

"How's your arm?"

Noah looked down at the bandages, barely able to see blood seeping through the gauze over the blue afterglow of the light bulb. "Fine."

"Two bullets in two days. I think that's a record. Where's my fucking boat?"

"In the chopper."

"Where's Hannah?"

"In my office. Brady fell asleep and she wanted to be there in case he woke up. Kid's going to have nightmares for months."

Cowboy leaned back in his chair. "If not years."

Noah sighed heavily. "I'm going back to the island."

"What for?"

"The people who killed her husband. When they came after us, they went looking at her place, first. I'll turn myself in to the cops as soon as I get back. I promise."

"That's right. I'm harboring a fugitive."

"I'll be gone in an hour."

"Hannah said she couldn't wait to get home. Does she know the tangos were looking for her?"

"No." Noah gulped down half the water in one long pull. "And you're not going to tell her."

Cowboy narrowed his eyes. "Who is she to you? On TV they called her your wife."

"The reporter just assumed and we didn't correct him. I was too busy begging her to come with me even though I'd kidnapped her and Brady at gunpoint." He explained the details of what happened.

"Do you care about her?"

"Fuck." He laughed without humor. "Ask me what you want to know, Leo."

"Did you sleep with her?"

"Yes."

"Do you love her?"

"It's only been a couple of days."

"I've seen it happen faster than that."

Noah thought of Brady and the tough road the boy had ahead of him. He thought of Hannah, starting from scratch after the waters receded, needing to get her family back to some semblance of normal. But try as he might, he couldn't picture himself in that scene, teetering noncommittally on the edge of their existence as Brady got more and more attached. He stared into space.

Don't forget. You're going to prison.

He shook his head. "No. I don't love her."

Cowboy said nothing, Noah's words seeming to echo in the space like a judge's final ruling. It was his decision to make and for all their sakes he had to make it a good one. He wasn't what they needed right now, no matter how much he wanted to be there.

"They're going to need someplace to stay," said Cowboy.

"Hawk offered them his house. He's going to Paris on the red-eye tonight." He stood. "I know what I'm doing, Cowboy."

"I'm sure you think you do."

"What the fuck is that supposed to mean?"

"I saw the way that kid looks at you. He worships you, man."

"That's not my fault."

"And her. Hannah." Cowboy stood and crossed his arms. "She looks at you like that, too. You and she are like mirror images of each other, staring all googly-eyed like you're on a damn Hallmark card."

"Like you said, we've been through a lot."

"And if it's more than that?"

"What's your fucking problem, huh? You playing cupid while I go to jail? You think that's what she wants? To get hooked up with somebody who's going to make her life even harder than it already is?"

"No."

"Because that's the shit I'm dealing with here. It doesn't matter if I care about her. It doesn't matter if I don't. All that matters is that I get the fuck out of here as soon as goddamn possible and Hannah and her kid stay here."

Movement in the open doorway of the conference room made him turn his head. There stood Hannah. She lifted her chin, her green eyes full of pain as she stared him down.

He opened his mouth to speak, but no words came out. She turned to Cowboy. "We're ready to go to Trevor's whenever you can take us. Brady's just using the washroom."

"Hannah," said Noah.

She lifted her hand. "Please don't."

"What I just said—"

"I really don't want to hear it. You and I both made our share of mistakes over the past few days. Let's just forget it ever happened."

"It's not what it sounded like," Noah said.

"It doesn't matter."

He crossed to her. "It does."

"Does it? Does it really?"

He was close enough to see her eyes were red, whether from fatigue or unshed tears he couldn't tell. "I didn't mean to hurt you."

She nodded and bit her lip, then lifted her chin once more. "You didn't hurt me. You saved us." She smiled and frowned at the same time. "Thank you, Noah. I'll always be grateful."

His throat worked. She was killing him, the grace with which she was handling this situation humbling. He wanted to open his arms and pull her close, smell the familiar scent of her hair, feel her body against his, but every word he'd said to Cowboy was true.

He had to get back to Hilton Head and find out who was after her. That was how best to love her right now. Instead of everything he wanted to say, he nodded and said, "You're welcome."

She turned and left the room, Brady's voice in the distance. "Where's Noah?"

"He's not coming, sweetie."

"But I want to see Noah!"

"Not tonight, baby. Come on."

Noah ripped his stare away from the empty conference room door, his vision unfocused.

"You're a bigger man than I am," said Cowboy. "Or a complete asshole, depending on how you want to look at it."

"I need Booger to come with me to the island. Logan, too."

"You can have Doc, but you'll have to talk to Booger yourself. He's still pissed about the last time."

25

Noah found Booger doing push-ups on the floor of the command center, the intricate tattoos on his muscled arms shiny with sweat. Noah rolled his eyes. Booger had been with HERO Force a couple of months already, but Noah had yet to figure out why anybody liked the asshole.

He was opinionated as fuck and as likely to do jumping jacks in front of a tango as to shoot the poor bastard. "We have to talk," said Noah.

Booger jumped to a stand, putting his hands on his hips. "What's up?"

"Logan and I are taking the chopper back to Hilton Head tonight. We've got at least one major asshole who's still breathing. Hannah and the kid are in danger."

"You should take Hawk."

"He's going to Paris."

"Then take Cowboy."

"I want you."

Booger narrowed his eyes. "Why?"

"Because you're quick on your feet and the best shot on the force, aside from me."

"We don't work well together."

"That's because you don't trust me."

Booger scoffed. "I don't trust you because you've demonstrated your inability to handle stress."

Noah stepped forward. "Bullshit. My sister had just died and you didn't trust me to do my damn job. You put our guys in jeopardy."

"Cowboy agreed with me. You were a goddamn mess."

Noah's hand clenched in a fist. "I could make the shot."

Booger shook his head. "Not a chance I was willing to take. There were kids involved."

"Fuck you." Noah punched him in the gut, Booger doubling over. "Come on, hit me," said Noah.

Booger came up with a left hook, catching Noah in the jaw, pain exploding like fireworks, and it felt good to finally get it out. He got Booger with a kidney punch and a head butt to the solar plexus, knocking the wind out of him with a whoosh.

"You've got a damn death wish," said Booger, his fist sinking into Noah's abs with great force. "You want me to stand up for you, fight next to you, you've got to deserve it."

Noah got him with a two-punch combination. "I'm fucking here, aren't I? Asking you for help? Telling you I need you on my six, damn it."

Booger pushed him back against the wall, and Noah used it as a springboard to attack him, pummeling him with his fists. Booger came back hard with another hook, making Noah see stars. "Fuck," said Noah, staggering away.

Booger was breathing hard. "Tell me what's different this time."

"I killed the bastard who shot my sister. That ghost isn't hanging off me the same way anymore."

"You're sure you can handle it?"

"I'm sure."

The sound of the men breathing was the only sound in the room for a long moment. "I'll go with you," said Booger.

"Logan's getting the chopper ready now. We leave in ten."

"Meet you there." Booger walked out of the room as Noah straightened, his fingers touching his bruised and battered face, coming away bloody.

He didn't see Brady hiding at the far side of the command center with Mr. Bojangles—determined to stay with his hero while his momma talked to Trevor. And when the boy retraced his steps to the helipad and stowed away on the chopper, neither of the men ever knew he was there.

26

H annah wiped her eyes and took in her reflection in the mirror. Thank God there was a ladies' room and no other women to use it, because she desperately needed to be alone, not wanting anyone to see her cry—least of all, Brady.

She told herself she'd just been through so much, the terrible stress of the last few days crashing down on her like a pile of boulders. But it was Noah's words that were her undoing, the callous things he said about needing to get away from her that truly broke her heart.

She should get out of here, make her way to Trevor's with Brady and settle in for the night, but her back had broken and there wasn't anything she could do to fix it until she climbed out from beneath these emotions.

You barely even know him. What do you care if he wants to leave?

But no matter how much she tried to let reason shine into the darkness, she refused to see the light. Her feelings for him had grown quickly in the time they'd been together, from her initial fear to burgeoning trust to something far, far deeper and more meaningful.

Love.

You're such a loser.

No one fell in love after two days! Jesus, it was probably Stockholm syndrome that had her so enamored with that bastard, not love.

Definitely not love.

She worked to get herself together, splashing water on her face and taking deep breaths until she only looked exhausted instead of emotionally devastated. The sound of a helicopter nearby made her shoulders shake. She'd never willingly go on one of those things again.

She looked at herself in the mirror one last time and exhaled with a great huff. She was ready. In her pocket she had the keys to Trevor's house and his address, along with some cash Leo had given her to get her through the next few weeks. It wasn't home, but it was close, and she just needed to hold herself together until she could get there.

You can do this.

She pushed out of the room and went in search of her son.

He wasn't in the kitchenette, where she'd left him with an orange soda and a straw, and she suspected he'd gone in search of Noah despite her expressly telling him not to.

Great. Now I'm going to have to face him again.

She made her way out the other side of the kitchenette and nearly ran into Cowboy. "Have you seen Brady?"

"No."

"He's probably with Noah. Where's his office?"

"Noah just left in the chopper."

She frowned. "I'm sure he's around here someplace."

"I'll help you look."

They searched HERO Force headquarters room by
room, calling for the boy. An hour and a half later she was
frantic—Brady still nowhere to be found. Cowboy called the
police to search the blocks around the building while he,
Hannah, and the new HERO Force recruits moved to other
floors in the building.

It was another forty minutes after that before one of the
recruits called Cowboy's cell phone. Hannah watched his
eyes go wide with concern before slamming into hers.

"What? Is he okay?" she asked.

"Thank you." He hung up the phone. "They found
Brady's stuffed bear on the helipad."

"On the roof?" she screamed, covering her mouth with
her hand. "What was he doing up there?" Understanding
dawned, a terrible realization. "No. No! He didn't. He
wouldn't!"

"I think he stowed away with Noah in the helicopter."
Cowboy checked his watch and cursed colorfully.

"Where were they going?"

"Hilton Head Island. They should be there by now."

She was hyperventilating, her chest rising and falling
too quickly. She clutched the wall as Cowboy made a
phone call.

"Get Doc on the radio. Brady is with them. Repeat, the
little boy is on the chopper. Do it now!"

It was her fault. She should have been watching him
instead of crying in the ladies' bathroom for twenty minutes
and leaving him alone. "Why did they go there? We
just left."

"The men who tried to kill you went to your apartment
before Noah's sister's. They're after you. Noah wanted to
stop them."

Her face crumpled. She knew what those men were like,

had seen what they were capable of, and now Brady was there without her. He was in danger. "My baby!"

His phone rang. "Did you get him?" He turned and kicked the wall with such force the drywall dented and she knew—the men had already gotten off the chopper. This was worse than when Joe died, time distorted, colors overly bright.

Then Cowboy gave her a fierce stare as he belted out loud, "Stefan, get me a pilot. I need to get to Hilton Head Island, stat."

27

"You need me," said Hannah, grabbing Cowboy's jumper. There was nowhere to land the plane and he was going to parachute down. It was already getting dark, her mind so confused by the passage of time she no longer knew what day it was. All she knew was she needed to get down on the ground and help find her son. "I know the building. I know where the condo is. I can get you to the hospital, to where I live. All of it."

"It isn't safe for you to come with me."

"I don't give a shit if it's safe! My baby is down there. He's got to be scared. He's the one who isn't safe. You have to let me come with you."

The very idea of what she was suggesting was ludicrous and she knew it. She wanted him to let her jump out of an airplane when she could barely tolerate the idea of air travel. But she would have swum through a lake-sized vat of lava if Brady was on the other side.

"I can't protect you, Hannah. You're a liability. You'll only slow me down."

She had to do something, had to find some way to

convince him. "The letter my husband wrote was addressed to three people. Joe knew one of them knew about the drug smuggling ring—was probably even in charge of it. Eric Manning was one of those three, but he insisted up until his death that he only allowed it to happen, he wasn't in charge."

"Which leaves two," said Cowboy.

"I know them both. Their names, their addresses. I worked with them for years."

"Tell me."

"Not unless you take me with you."

"Fuck." He shook his head. "This is a very dangerous game you're playing."

She knew Cowboy had no way to reach Noah now that he was out of the chopper and away from its radio. Cell phone service hadn't been restored. She had the information he needed to find Noah and Brady.

They were playing chicken, staring at each other as the plane shot through the sky toward her child.

He relented. "Get a jumpsuit on. Over there. You ever jump out of a plane before?"

"No."

He cursed again. "Then you'll come with me, tandem." He moved to the skydiving equipment in a large crate, handing her a jumpsuit and goggles and changing out his harness. "You have to hurry. We don't have a lot of time until we're over the drop zone."

Cowboy wasn't kidding. No sooner did she get the suit on than he was rigging up her harness and barking orders on how to hold her body, which would be strapped directly to his. She didn't let herself think about what she was about to do, focusing only on her son's face as the green light lit and the side of the fuselage opened to the dark sky.

She stepped with Cowboy's steps. He tapped her shoulder three times and pushed her forward, jumping out of the plane. She closed her throat against the scream that wanted to come up and closed her eyes. There was only Brady's face.

Brady's face—and Noah's.

28

Noah grabbed the inflatable motorboat and hopped out of the chopper behind Booger. They'd landed on top of Hannah's apartment complex just after the sun set, armed and ready to face whatever came their way.

"You sure you want me to leave the bird here?" asked Logan. He was there as a pilot only, since he'd broken his femur in a skydiving accident that had nearly killed him. The fact that he could work the chopper's pedals at all was a testament to how far he'd come.

"We might need to get out in a hurry," said Booger.

"Fine, but I'm getting out. No sense in sitting in a giant helicopter that screams, 'We're here. You can shoot us now.'"

"You can sit inside the stairwell," said Noah. "Got your firearm?"

"No, I left it back at headquarters with my knitting needles. What the fuck, you think I broke my leg and I lost my balls, too?"

"Just checking up on you, Doc."

Noah led the way into the stairwell, the smell of stank

water and mold assaulting his nose. Logan might be better off in the chopper.

He held his weapon at the ready, not expecting to encounter trouble but prepared for it anyway. His high-powered long-range rifle was strapped to his back, just in case. The tangos had been here once already but that didn't mean they wouldn't come back, and God only knows how far away they'd be when they finally found them.

Logan stayed at the top of the stairs as the other men made their way to the third floor and Hannah's apartment. The door was wide open, the carpeting soaked, with glass shards littered everywhere. Noah checked the bedrooms and bath. "All clear."

Booger pulled out a map and opened it on the coffee table. "Where are we going first?"

Noah pointed. "The hospital. A quarter-mile to our west. I want to go through the offices of the two administrators in question and see if we can pinpoint our tango, then go from there."

"Agreed."

They went downstairs—the water clearly lower than it had been when Noah was last here—and inflated the boat with the CO$_2$ cartridge. The moon provided ample light to navigate, and he remembered the route he'd taken with Hannah. They arrived at the hospital without incident and entered the building, a portrait of the chief administrator hanging in the lobby.

"That's Patel," Noah said. "The head honcho. Hannah said the other one is thinner and bald. A white guy."

They headed directly for the offices on the second floor. Booger was the first to reach the chief administrator's office, stopping in his tracks as he peered inside. "I found Patel."

Noah caught up and looked inside. Sure enough, the

man from the lobby portrait was dead on the floor with a bullet wound to his head. "He wasn't here yesterday."

"Which means someone's been in here since you left."

"And maybe they're still inside." Noah's mind went into overdrive. "If Patel was in charge of the drug ring, he could have been killed by one of his men." The sheer number of people involved was enough to make his head spin. "There were three or four guys at the medical supply truck the night of the hurricane, plus the cop. Six at Lizzie's apartment yesterday. The numbers are staggering for this kind of operation."

"Maybe they work for the medical supply company," said Booger. "It could be a front. How big is the drug operation?"

"Hundreds of thousands of dollars a year. But that's the hospital's value. The street cost would be much higher." He narrowed his eyes. "Lincare. The name on the truck was Lincare Medical Supply." He stepped around Patel's body and into the office. "Help me look through files. Anything you can find on Lincare."

The men searched all of his office and his secretary's file cabinet as well. "Over here," said Booger, pulling a file from Patel's desk drawer and opening it on the desk.

"It's a ledger," said Noah, his eyes scanning the numbers and abbreviated transaction descriptions. "All handwritten." He flipped through the pages, names atop each one. On a hunch, he searched for the one that might secure his freedom. "Buchanan," he said, finding it. "The cop who shot me. This proves he was involved in the drug operation."

"Who does business like this today?" asked Booger. "Everything's computerized."

"Accounting is, for sure," said Noah. "Patel was keeping these records by hand so no one else would see them. If you were stealing boatloads of money, you'd probably use paper and pen, too."

"But if Patel was in charge of the drug scheme, who killed Patel?"

"Someone from the medical supply company. The men from the truck, who I'm willing to bet were the same men in black who attacked us at my sister's condo."

"How are we going to find them?"

"We don't have to find them. They're already looking for us. We just have to let them know we're here."

"The helicopter," said Booger.

No sense in sitting in a giant helicopter that screams, 'We're here. You can shoot us now.'

Noah was already moving. "Fuck. Logan's by himself."

The men ran to the stairs and down as quickly as they could. They'd just exited the building when three gunshots echoed in the night. Booger hopped in the boat and reached to start the engine.

"Wait!" said Noah. "They're trying to draw us out."

"And it's working. Get in the damn boat."

"If they're by the chopper, they'll have a clear line of sight to the boat as we make our way back. We're dead in the water, Booger. Literally."

"What the fuck do you suggest? We just sit back and let them kill Logan?"

"The roof. Come on!" Noah turned and ran back into the hospital, his arms pumping as he raced to the stairwell and climbed to the top. This was where Eric Manning fell to his death, Lizzie's condo visible in the distance. "Stay low." He got to the knee wall and slipped his sniper's rifle from his back, fitting it with a night vision scope and setting it on its tripod.

He peered through the scope, his entire world

suddenly standing on end as the people on the rooftop came into focus. "Jesus Christ." There was no denying what he was seeing, no way to make sense of the horror in front of him, and he felt physically sick with fear. "Two men with guns. Three hostages. Brady, Hannah, and Cowboy."

"How the fuck did they get here? Where's Doc?"

"I don't see him." Cowboy was off to the side, but Hannah and Brady were sandwiched between tangos. "Fucking Christ. How can I get a shot?"

"Careful, Ryker."

"Don't you think I know that?" he screamed, forcing himself to focus and regulate his breathing. The slightest movement could throw everything off.

This was the scene Booger had been trying to avoid. That last mission when Cowboy took him off the gun because he was so fucked up about Lizzie's death. There were kids involved.

Kids involved.

Brady was over there. Sweet little Brady, the boy he loved. Hannah would never forgive him if he hurt her son. Hell, he'd never forgive himself.

"You don't have to do this," said Booger. "We can go over there and deal with it face-to-face."

"We'll be dead. That's what they're hoping for. No. This is our chance."

"Can you make this shot, Noah?"

"It's not even a quarter-mile away. Basic."

"Basic doesn't have a little kid in harm's way."

Sweat dripped into Noah's mouth and he licked it away. He could do this. He had to do this. They were counting on him to be his best. A steely determination settled between his shoulder blades. The tango closest to Brady had to go first, but he would have only moments to get the second one.

He lined up his first shot and fired. The tango fell, the adults scattering. He lined up the sight on the second tango, but he pulled Brady in front of him, using the boy like a shield.

"You should have picked Hannah, fuckface. She's taller."

Just as Noah fired a shot over Brady's head, the tango moved and Noah feared he'd shot the boy, too. Every cell in his body held still while he watched the tango fall to the ground, Brady seemingly unharmed.

Noah dropped his head to his chest, breathing hard once more. "Thank God."

"You got them?"

"Yeah."

"Never doubted you for a minute," said Booger.

They found Logan swimming in the fetid water, halfway to the hospital, and pulled him into the boat. He'd managed to get away and was coming to alert Noah and Booger, enormous leg cast and all.

He told them how Cowboy had parachuted in with Hannah shortly after they left, finding the boy safely asleep in the chopper.

Logan had needed to sit down, finding a comfortable spot on the other side of the large HVAC unit. That's when their company arrived. The men didn't see him and he managed to escape back into the stairwell.

"You did good, Doc," said Noah.

Booger slapped Logan on the back. "Hell yeah."

They reached the condo, Noah hopping out and leaving Booger to help Logan back up the stairs. "I've got to get—"

Booger waved him on. "Go. I've got this."

Noah took the steps two at a time all the way to the top,

pushing out the exit door with a rush. Hannah and Brady were sitting in the chopper and he slowly made his way to them.

"Noah!" said Brady. Blood dripped down the side of his face.

Noah nearly fell to his knees, realizing how close he'd come to hurting the boy. "Are you okay?" Noah climbed inside, the boy wrapping himself around him.

"I got a cut from the bad man. Mom is going to fix it."

"Let me see."

The boy had in fact been grazed by a bullet—one from Noah's own gun. He frowned and met Hannah's eyes. "Will you let me help?"

She nodded. "I don't have my medical bag."

He found the first aid kit. Hannah held out her hand, taking it from him. "You have the harder job." A small smile settled onto her lips as she looked from Noah to her son.

She's letting me comfort him.

He was stunned.

Brady scurried onto his lap. "Wait," said Noah. "Ear protection first." The headset was in the way of the wound, so Noah fitted the boy with earplugs, taking a pair himself so the two of them matched. Brady clung to him, waiting for his mother to begin.

It felt so good to hold him again after their ordeal, his fear that he would end the life of the people he most wanted to save. He thought of how close he had come to truly hurting Brady, and his eyes stung as emotion poured through him, thick and all consuming. Now it was he who clung to the boy while Hannah bandaged his wound, so grateful they were alive. Hannah and Brady had become more important to him in a short while than he would have thought possible.

Booger and Cowboy climbed into the cabin and Logan into the cockpit, donning their ear protection and settling into their seats. Booger leaned back and pulled a baseball cap over his eyes. Cowboy met Noah's stare and nodded once.

Noah knew then he and Cowboy would make peace. He'd apologize to Cowboy and be allowed back onto HERO Force, forgiven—assuming Noah was able to exonerate himself. Cowboy leaned back and closed his eyes.

As the chopper took off from Hilton Head Island, Noah knew for the first time he was truly leaving his sister behind. Grief was sharp, his tears that had first collected for Brady now mingling with the grief in his heart. He gave in to them, allowing them to drip from his eyes as they'd longed to do for so long.

Lizzie was gone and nothing would change that, but he'd found out the truth of what had happened to her and the men who'd killed her were dead. He had done everything that could be done. His work here was complete.

I miss you, sis.

The tears were cathartic, forcing him to feel the helplessness he'd tried to avoid, the pain. He stroked Brady's back, his small body warm and heavy and comforting as he cried.

Hannah finished her work and sat beside them, opening her arms. Noah leaned into her, smelling her scent, knowing she could feel his tears against her chest and not caring. She knew everything that was in his heart at this moment and if she thought less of him for his reaction, then that was too damn bad.

She and Brady formed a protective cocoon around Noah, a hard exoskeleton for the weakness in the middle. They stayed that way until the storm inside him passed, the sun breaking through the clouds that had threatened him for far too long. He sat up. "Thank you," he mouthed, knowing she couldn't hear him.

She kissed him full on the mouth, surprising him. He looked to Cowboy, then Brady, finding them both asleep, and kissed her back, deeply. By the time he lifted his head, his breathing was speeding up and he thought better of continuing to kiss her.

Their eyes met, hers bright green and shining with emotion. He ran his finger down the side of her face, then leaned back and opened his arm. She snuggled into his side, close to her son.

Noah wouldn't let himself think of the future right now. It was enough just to experience this moment, and he knew he'd remember it for the rest of his life, no matter what happened when they reached Atlanta. He kissed the top of her head, his eyelids suddenly heavy, and fell asleep with a smile.

29

Trevor Hawkins didn't speak French, which made the trip from the airport to the movie set some two hours outside Paris a royal pain in the ass.

He was tired from flying all night on the cramped airplane, stuck in the middle seat and barely able to sleep. He would have crashed in the taxi, but the driver was determined to make conversation despite how hard it was to communicate, leaving Hawk to repeat, "I don't want to talk anymore," over and over again, which served only to make the driver laugh and talk faster.

The diamond ring in his pocket was heavy on his mind. He and Olivia had been talking about marriage for a while now. They even had a timeline—after she finished this movie—but he hadn't gotten down on one knee and she wasn't wearing his ring. He'd wanted something special, something worthy of a Hollywood starlet, and that had taken him some time. Now that the time was here, he couldn't wait to put it on her finger.

And make love like rabbits.

Just the thought had his dick waking up. She'd been gone too long and he missed the fuck out of that woman.

"*Savez-vous de quoi je parle?*" asked the cabbie, who'd been chattering on while Trevor thought about a naked Olivia beckoning him into bed.

"I don't want to talk anymore!"

The cabbie laughed hysterically.

It was past noon by the time they reached the set, hundreds of people milling about or running around, but no sign of Olivia. He groaned and pulled his English-French electronic translator from his pocket once more.

Brooke Barrons definitely got a reaction, but it took him a while to explain who he was and to actually get directions to her dressing room. Even as he was grateful, he shook his head at the ease with which he accomplished that task. No wonder she didn't feel safe here.

He doubted there was anything to really be concerned about, but if she was worried, then he would be here for her, acting as her personal bodyguard for the duration of the film.

And I will like it.

He smiled all the way to her dressing room. Maybe she would have time right now and they could make love before she returned to the set. Her name was on the door, another no-no for someone who wanted to be left alone, and he shook his head. He knocked, the door opening a small crack.

"Olivia?" He pushed it open to reveal a space about fifteen feet square. It was messy, which instantly struck him as odd, then his heart began to pick up speed as he looked more closely. There was makeup scattered on the floor. Jewelry, too. A handheld mirror was shattered, bits of glass shining up from the carpet.

Trevor moved into the bathroom, calling her name, though he already feared she wasn't here, his mind going into overdrive as he imagined what might have happened. He tried to think of rational explanations. She'd been upset. Maybe she was throwing things.

Then he saw her cell phone and purse sitting on a side table, the hair on the back of his neck going up. She never would have left those here with the door open. Not on purpose, anyway.

A hulking fat man appeared in the doorway, a sandwich in his hand. "*Qui es-tu?*" demanded the man.

Hawk didn't need a translator for that one but asked a question of his own. "Where is Brooke Barrons?"

The man looked around the room as if only now realizing she wasn't there. "I don't know," he said in heavily accented English.

"Are you her security detail?"

The man looked at him blankly.

"Her bodyguard?" he clarified.

"*Oui*, bodyguard."

Hawk crossed to him. "Then where is she?"

The man shrugged.

"Where the hell were you?"

He held up his sandwich. "Lunch."

30

Hannah closed the bedroom door and made her way back to Noah's living room. Brady had woken up after the helicopter flight and stayed awake while they drove to Noah's house outside Atlanta. They'd never even had a chance to bring their things to Trevor's, which made it easy enough to change her mind when Noah asked her to stay.

The whole way here she'd worked to keep her mind quiet and her questions about their future at bay. Tonight she would let herself love this man and feel loved in return, no matter what came after.

Anticipation made her jumpy. Longing flushed her cheeks.

From the outside the house looked like a modest ranch, but the inside resembled a wooded cabin, with high-peaked ceilings, knotty pine, and dark beams. It was beautiful and it suited him perfectly.

She stepped into the room. "He's asleep."

Noah sat in a big leather chair, his legs stretched out on

an ottoman and a bottle of beer in his hand. "Do you want something to drink? Or if you're tired we can go to bed."

"I'll take a beer." He moved to get up and she waved him back down. "I'm up. I'll get it." She found the fridge and reached for a bottle, belatedly realizing she didn't even want one.

She did want to go to bed, though, but it wasn't fatigue that was driving her decision. She bit her lip and went back to Noah. "Let's go to bed."

"Okay." He finished his beer and came with her, leading the way down the dark hallway to the bedroom at the end. He turned the light on, a king-sized bed drawing her attention and holding it. She clenched her hands in front of her.

"I'm sorry," he said. "I should have...I guess I just assumed..."

She looked at him and smiled. "I want to sleep with you."

"Good." He moved toward her, opening his arms. "I want to sleep with you, too."

She touched his cheek gently. "What happened to your face?"

"I owed Booger an apology."

"And this is it?"

"Pretty much." His stare focused on her mouth.

She lifted her head for his kiss, the light scent of beer teasing her nose. He slipped his hand under her shirt and up her back, the feel of his fingers on her skin so good she moaned. "Turn off the light."

He did as she asked, coming back to her and lifting her in his arms. He laid her on the bed, pulling his shirt over his head before moving beside her. In the darkness she could just make out the shape of his body, his muscles calling out to her to be touched, and she let her hands stroke every inch of exposed skin before unbuckling his pants and moving lower.

"I want to see you," he said, again slipping his hand beneath her shirt and pulling it up past her bra. He touched her breasts through the fabric. "So beautiful," he whispered before bending his head, kissing the skin over her heart and the globes peeking out of the lace.

She reached around to her back, unhooking her bra, and he pulled it down, nuzzling her bare nipple before taking it in his mouth. She bucked against him.

She was beyond foreplay, beyond needing this level of care tonight. She wanted to feel him filling her up, making her body come alive, and she stripped off her pants and underwear, eager hands pulling at his clothes until he was as naked as she.

He kissed down her abdomen, his hand moving between her legs, and she spread them wide for him to enter. One single kiss on her clitoris and she knew she'd never be able to hold out. "I need you inside me when I come." His fingers thrust deep into her body and she gasped, so close to orgasm from that one single move, her body clutching him tightly.

"Jesus, Hannah." He pulled out, fumbling at the bedside table, the tear of the condom packet like music to her ears. Then he was on top of her, that glorious cock pushing inside her heat, filling her up with everything she needed.

She moved beneath him, matching him stroke for stroke, desperate to become one with this man. She flipped him over and rode him hard, loving the feel of him inside her, the sounds of pleasure he made as she fucked him, his hands on her hips pulling her onto him faster.

She took his hands and held them over his head, kissing him with her tongue as she moved her hips at her own pace.

She slid slowly up and down his thick, throbbing shaft, tormenting him as much as herself, until she couldn't wait anymore and picked up speed. Her orgasm ripped through her, hips freezing as sensation overwhelmed her body.

Noah pushed her onto her back and drove into her, drawing out her climax and intensifying it, her entire body tingling from the explosion of sensation. The slap of his balls against her was loud, his face determined as he forced himself as deep as he could inside her and cried out with his own release.

He collapsed on top of her.

I could get used to this.

Oh, man, she really could. Sharing a house with this man. Sharing his bed night after night until their bodies were worn out from loving.

But what about Brady?

She could take chances with her own heart but not with his. He was already too attached to Noah, and while she understood it, she couldn't allow it to continue unless Noah was going to stay in their lives.

"Stay with me," Noah said, and she frowned as if he'd read her thoughts. "I'm greedy," he said. "I want days with you to do anything we want." He pushed up on his arms. "I want time, Hannah. I just made love to you and I can feel you pulling away."

"Brady already loves you."

"I love him, too."

I love you, too.

She wouldn't allow herself to say the words. It was too soon. Ridiculous to think the feelings were real.

But isn't that the problem?

The feelings couldn't be real. They were a byproduct of what they'd been through; there was no way they could last.

And while she would gladly take any moment she could with Noah by her side—feeling this way about him—it wasn't fair to put Brady through the same thing.

"I love you, too, Hannah."

She pushed him off of her. "You're heavy."

"That's it? I tell you I love you and you tell me I'm heavy?"

She licked her lips, wishing this conversation could have been held at bay, willing to do anything to have the whole night in his arms before needing to protect herself from these words. "It's an illusion. It isn't real."

"How can you say that?"

"We were fighting for our lives. We had to rely on each other."

"I do that shit all the time. I've never told anyone I loved them before."

"Never?"

"No."

She wanted so desperately to believe it, to make it be true, but nothing he could say would be able to convince her. Her eyes stung and she needed to get away from him before he could see, before he could console her and give her yet another reason to cling to his side. She sat up and pulled her shirt over her head.

"Are you leaving?" he asked.

"I'm going to sleep with Brady."

"Stay with me," he said again.

"No." Her voice broke and she hated that he could hear it. She pulled on her panties and her pants, scurrying from the room in the darkness.

31

The water receded. It took some time, but Hilton Head Island was slowly getting back to normal. The hospital reopened first, then the businesses and schools. Hannah bought a new car to replace the one she'd lost in the storm and made a new plan for her life.

A plan that didn't include her son growing up without her.

She gave her notice at work after the initial crisis had passed and began looking for jobs in private practice. They wouldn't pay as well as her surgical position at the hospital —at least for starters—but being in debt no longer seemed like much of a threat to her well-being.

Eventually Brady stopped asking about Noah and when they would see him again, though he'd given Mr. Bojangles a toy gun so the bear could help keep them safe. And as Hurricane Sylvester crossed the Caribbean and set its sights on the Carolina coast, Hannah was ready to weather the storm. It wasn't forecasted to be a direct hit, but this time she was prepared for anything.

Or so she thought.

She sent Brady with his grandparents in the RV just to be safe, knowing the boy would have a good time, then stopped by the corner store for bread, milk, and ice cream before heading home alone.

That was the part that surprised her. With the storm coming, her mind was filled with Noah even more than it usually was, and she missed him acutely. Her life had been forever changed when a stranger with a bullet wound made her take him home and stitch him up, and she wanted him back in her life more than she would have thought possible.

The feelings hadn't gone away as she'd predicted—if anything they'd gotten stronger. She ate her ice cream with the lights off, watching the rain hit the windows, thunder rumbling in the distance.

The last time there'd been a hurricane coming she should have left but had nowhere to go, and this time she could certainly stay but there was only one place in the world she wanted to be. She put down her bowl and grabbed her cell phone. "I can't believe I'm doing this."

Opening her browser, she searched for HERO Force.

A knock on the door made her start. "Coming." She pulled it open.

Noah stood on the other side.

"I heard you were getting a hurricane," he said.

She was dumbfounded that he was here, her eyes wide and her stomach suddenly in knots. "It's going to miss us."

"I know. I wanted to see you."

She swallowed against the knot that had suddenly tightened in her throat. "I wanted to see you, too."

He looked at her hungrily, his hair dripping into his eyes, then peered over her shoulder. "Is Brady here?"

"He's with my in-laws. I know it's not going to be that bad, but after the last time, it seemed like the right thing to do." She stepped back, holding the door open for him to enter, his height and wide shoulders seeming to fill up the room.

He took off his wet jacket. "I didn't come all this way because of the weather report."

"You said that already," she said stupidly, her toes curling into the rug.

"I came to tell you you were wrong." He walked toward her, his eyes dark and dangerous, making her think of a predatory cat. "It wasn't an illusion," he said. "It's real. As real as anything I've ever experienced. I love you, Hannah, and those feelings aren't going to go away today or tomorrow or anytime soon."

She smiled. "I know."

"You do?"

She nodded. "I was just calling HERO Force to see if they'd give me your number."

"You were?" He grinned wickedly. "Tell me why."

The words were on the tip of her tongue but still she hesitated. Speaking them was the beginning of something new, but it also meant letting go of a piece of her past. Joe couldn't be the only man in her heart anymore. "Because I love you, too."

He reached for her, and she all but climbed him like a tree. Their mouths met in a hungry kiss, her arms wrapping around him, holding him to her.

"I can't believe you came back here," she said.

"I can't believe I waited as long as I did." He kept kissing her, his mouth barely leaving her lips to speak. "Were you really calling HERO Force just now?"

"Yes."

He growled. "Take off your clothes."

She pulled them off as quickly as she could, dropping them to the floor as Noah did the same.

He'd come back to her after all this time without him, and her heart swelled with joy. Life had already given her one man to love, and now it was giving her another. She couldn't compare Joe to Noah and she knew she didn't need to. Each love was its own, each man meeting her needs in a completely different way.

She took him into her bed and loved him with her body as she loved him in her heart, bringing him inside of her and showing him that joy. When their bodies were satisfied and tired, she snuggled in the crook of his arm and told him about the changes she was making in her life and the gun-toting stuffed bear. Brady would be so happy to see this man.

Noah rubbed her shoulder. "I was exonerated in Buchanan's death, Hannah. I'm not going to prison."

She kissed his chest. "I never believed you would."

"I want to date you."

She smiled. "Okay."

"I live four hours away. Do you think I could stay here sometimes to see you?"

"You can stay here anytime you like."

"Are you worried about Brady?"

"Only a little. I want to be with you and I don't expect that to change. It's not a bad thing for him to see his momma in love."

"I love him, too, you know."

"I know." She closed her eyes, his chest hair tickling her cheek. "I'll try my best to share him with you."

Noah kissed her head. "I'll keep him safe. I promise."

She smiled against his skin, remembering every time Joe had said those words. "I believe you will."

32

Dear Santa,

For Christmas I want a dog. My mom said I can have one and Noah said it's okay with him. I don't want anything else because I already got a bulletproof vest for Mr. Bojangles for my birthday so I'm all set. A big dog with spots who likes to play.

Thank you.

Brady

P.S.

I want dog treats too. And toys.

For the dog, not me.

P.S.2.

And a GI Joe for Noah.

Printed in Great Britain
by Amazon

25731463R00098